POKÉMON
ADVENTURES

Pokémon ADVENTURES
Volume 1
Perfect Square Edition

Story by **HIDENORI KUSAKA**
Art by **MATO**

English Adaptation/Gerard Jones
Translation/Kaori Inoue
Miscellaneous Text Adaptation/Ben Costa
Touch-up & Lettering/Wayne Truman
Design/Sean D. Williams
Editor, 1st Edition/William Flanagan
Editor, Perfect Square Edition/Annette Roman

Printed in the U.S.A.

Published by VIZ Media, LLC
P.O. Box 77010
San Francisco, CA 94107

16
First printing, June 2009
Sixteenth printing, January 2018

www.perfectsquare.com

www.viz.com

POKéMON
TM
ADVENTURES
1
VOLUME ONE
Story by Hidenori Kusaka
Art by Mato

CONTENTS

IN A PLACE CALLED PALLET TOWN...
FOOEY! IT BOUNCED OFF AGAIN!
MY TURN, MY TURN!
D'YOU REALLY THINK YOU'VE GOT A CHANCE?
RRRNN
OH, BE QUIET.
I'M GONNA CATCH THIS POKÉMON... AND MAKE IT MY PERSONAL PET!
WATCH THIS!
IF YOU WANT TO CATCH A POKÉMON...
...FIRST YOU'VE GOTTA WEAKEN IT... THEN THROW THE POKÉ BALL.
TSK TSK
HUH ?
BONNG
I-IT B-BOUNCED OFF...?
HAHAHA! YOU CAN'T CATCH A POKÉMON LIKE THAT!

1 A Glimpse of the Glow
F'RINSTANCE... TRY THIS!
GO, POLIWHIRL!
VMM
DORRR?
?!
BLASH
B-SHOO
GIVE IT THE WATER GUN!
AN' NOW THAT NIDORINO'S WEAK, I THROW THE POKÉ BALL AND...
PON!
YEAH!
IT LOOKS DIZZY!
WOW!

HA HA! GOTCHA, NIDORINO!
BON
NIGGLE RIGGLE
THAT WAS GREAT, RED!
HEH HEH HEH!
COOL!
EVERYBODY KNOWS ME IN PALLET TOWN. AND WHY NOT?
I'M THE BEST POKÉMON TRAINER AROUND!
HUH? WHAT ARE POKÉMON, YOU ASK?
STRANGE CREATURES THAT LIVE IN THE FORESTS AND LAKES.

I DON'T KNOW HOW MANY KINDS OF POKÉMON THERE ARE IN THE WORLD...
BUT I KNOW I'M GONNA CATCH 'EM ALL!
HEY, RED— DO YOU KNOW PROFESSOR OAK?
THE OLD GUY AT THE EDGE OF TOWN?
WHAT ABOUT THAT WEIRDO?
WELL...
PEOPLE SAY HE KNOWS A WHOLE LOT ABOUT POKÉMON.
MAYBE HE CAN TEACH US A THING OR TWO ABOUT HOW TO CATCH THEM...
YOU DON'T NEED THAT OLD NUT.
I'LL TEACH YOU EVERYTHING YOU NEED TO KNOW.
MAY-BE...
BUT THEY SAY PROFESSOR OAK TAUGHT HIS GRANDSON TO BE ONE OF THE WORLD'S GREATEST POKÉMON TRAINERS...
HIS GRAND-SON?!
YEAH. HE'S BEEN STUDYING OVERSEAS FOR A LONG TIME. HE JUST GOT BACK.
HMPH!!
I DON'T CARE WHO HE IS—HE DOESN'T STAND A CHANCE AGAINST ME!!

FOR SURE!
SEE YOU TOMORROW!
SEE YA!
HMM...
OLD PROFESSOR OAK, HUH...?
VOMP
OOMF!
HEY!
WATCH IT, YOU WORM!
EEP!
WH-WHERE'D THOSE GUYS COME FROM?
TROMP TROMP

HEY!
THOSE ARE POKÉ BALLS!
KSH KSH KSH KSH
THEY'VE GOTTA BE POKÉMON TRAINERS.
IT MUST BE HIDING IN THE GENERAL AREA!!
DO NOT REST UNTIL YOU FIND IT!
ZHH
FIND THE PHANTOM POKÉMON!!
"PHAN-TOM POKÉ-MON"?
NEVER HEARD OF IT!
WE HAVEN'T SEARCHED THE WEST WOOD YET!
ZHH
COMB IT TO THE LAST BLADE!!
ZHH
ZHH

THAT PHANTOM POKÉMON IS GONNA BE *MINE*... OR MY NAME'S NOT RED!
KSH
KSH
THANKS FOR THE TIP, GUYS!
...
HEH HEH HEH
VWIP
VWIP
GREAT... THEY DIDN'T GET HERE YET.
WHERE *AAARE* YOU, LI'L PHANTOM POKÉMON...?
WOBBLE
BOP
HUH? WH... WHAT'S...
...THAT ?!
THE WEST WOOD ...

ONE O' THOSE CREEPS BEAT ME TO IT!!
KCH
AND WHO'S THAT?!
CHAR-MANDER, GO!!
NOW!
BOOM
!
CHOOSH!
A POKÉ-MON!
HE'S A POKÉMON TRAINER!

BZZZXXT
CHOOSH!
KRAK!
YEEESH... I'VE NEVER SEEN A POKéMON BATTLE LIKE THIS.
HIS POKéMON... THAT'S A CHAR-MANDER.
BUT... WHAT'S THAT GLOWING CREATURE?!
I'VE NEVER SEEN ANYTHING LIKE IT!
WELL... GO, CHAR-MANDER!
BEAT THAT THING!
...
BZZT
BZZT
BZZT

ENOUGH!
CHARMANDER, RETURN!
WHAT THE—?!
PWIK
BON!
SHWRRRR R
PAPF!
WHAT ARE YOU DOING?!
YOU ALMOST HAD IT, YOU, YOU—!!
KSH
...
HMF!

MY TURN!! GO, POLIWHIRL!!
BON!
WATER GUN!!
BSH
!
GLEEM
BASH!
?!
ACK!
BWOMP!
POLI-WHIRL?!
VWRR
EEE!

POLIWHIRL! C-COME ON, SNAP OUT OF IT, BUDDY!
...
ARE YOU BLIND?
DIDN'T YOU NOTICE ANYTHING WHILE YOU WERE WATCHING US FIGHT...?
I COULD TELL RIGHT AWAY THAT THERE WAS A VAST DIFFERENCE IN STRENGTH.
THAT'S WHY I STOPPED THE FIGHT.
KNOW YOUR LIMITATIONS. OR YOU'LL ONLY BEAT YOURSELF.
REMEMBER THAT.
HEH HEH HEH
SHFF...
Y'MEAN I...I ACTUALLY... ***LOST?***

HWUUUUUU
!
!
THE FIELD...?
IT'S ALL BURNED UP! WHAT HAPPENED HERE?!
!
ANSWER ME, WORM!! WHAT HAVE YOU DONE?!
IGNORE HIM! THE MEW IS WHAT COUNTS!
IT MIGHT STILL BE NEARBY!!
GO!!
ZHH
ZHH
ZH ZH!
...

SO THIS IS OL' PROF. OAK'S LAB...
SHHP
OAK POKÉMON RESEARCH LAB
THEY SAY HE'S A MEAN OLD GEEZER...
...SO I ALWAYS KEPT AWAY...
BUT I GUESS THE ONLY PLACE I'LL LEARN TO BE A GREAT POKÉMON TRAINER...
...IS HERE.
TREMMBLLL
BINGBONNNG!
GLMMP

BING BONG
BONGBING
BINNNG
ANY-BODY HOME?
HUH?! IT'S OPEN!
KRIIII—
!
2 Bulbasaur, Come Home!

OH... W- WOW...
VWIP
I HAD NO IDEA THERE WERE SO MANY POKÉMON...
VWIP
?
WHAT'S THIS ONE?
ffp
"BULB... A... SAUR."
IT HAS A BUD ON ITS BACK! COOL!
BULBASAUR
LOOK AT THIS, POLIWHIRL!
BLLLB
SSSR SSSR SSSR

EH?
KRI!
WH-
WH-
WH-
?!
NO!
YOU
IDIOT
!!
WAAA...
TRIP!
KLIK!
W...WAIT!
N-NO...
I M-MEAN
I...
YOU...
YOU...
POKÉ-
THIEF
!
DOMP
DOMP
PSHHHHHHH
B-B-BOING!
EE-
YAAAA
!

VIII—IIIN
I D-DIDN'T MEAN TO...
NOW LOOK WHAT YOU'VE DONE!!
YUK..
GRRRR
BL ECH!
OKAY !!
WOG
WOG
VNN
VIN
JUST GET THEM BACK !
DON'T...TELL ME...THAT SOME OF THEM...HUFF... ESCAPED.
HUFFF... HUFF... UHHH...
LATER (MUCH LATER)...
HOW... MANY MORE... ?

OUCH!
BUT WE'VE GOTTA GET 'EM BACK, OR...
BUT I'M NOT A...! I'M SORRY I CAME INTO YOUR POKÉMON LAB UNINVITED... I'M SORRY I LET YOUR POKÉMON LOOSE!
I-I'LL GO OUT AN' GET 'EM!
VMM
HEY!
OHHHH, NO YOU DON'T— POKÉ-THIEF!
IT'S TOO LATE FOR THAT...
IT'LL BE DARK BEFORE WE FIND THEM ALL.
WE CAN'T JUST GIVE UP!
I'M GOING AFTER 'EM!
...
YOU THINK YOU CAN DO IT ALL BY YOUR-SELF?
YOU WON'T KNOW WHAT TO LOOK FOR!
CHING-CHING!
CHING CHING
AND AFTER WE GET THEM ALL BACK, YOU'D BETTER BELIEVE...
...THAT I'M TURNING YOU IN!!
VSSH
YES, SIR!

HERE, KITTY, KITTY...
VIRIDIAN CITY
NOW!
BON!
GOTCHA!
ONLY ONE LEFT...
PHEW... IF I'D KNOWN I'D BE CHASING THEM ALL THE WAY TO VIRIDIAN CITY, I'D HAVE DECIDED I'M TOO OLD FOR THIS...
THE LAST ONE IS BULBASAUR.
THERE IT IS!!
YES... B-BUT THAT ONE...
EEP?
VMM
IT'S GOING IN THERE!
VIRIDIAN CITY GYM
CLOSED

YEESH!
GYM
WHERE WOULD IT GO...?
KRIII-
HURRY!
VSH
VIRIDIAN CITY GYM
CLOSED
COME TO DADDY, LITTLE...
OH-HO-HO. THERE YOU ARE.
NOW, REALLY! I'M YOUR TRAINER...!
SRRR
DOMP
OOG

...
OF COURSE YOU'RE NERVOUS...
IT'S THE FIRST TIME YOU'VE BEEN OUTSIDE!
VIP
BLB?
DON'T BE AFRAID, BULBASAUR.
...
I'LL BET YOU'VE NEVER SEEN ANOTHER LIVING THING BESIDES THE OL' PROF, *HUH?*
YOU WERE KEPT SEPARATE FROM THE OTHERS IN THE POKÉMON LAB, WEREN'T YOU?
!!
KRI-
?!
...
YEAH, THAT'S A GOOD BOY. ARE YOU HUNGRY?
PRRRR PRRRR

GASP!
I-IT'S...
A WILD MACHOKE !!
MMMMAAAA
YAA !!
VOO
SSSRRRR
CHKK
BLLLL

PROF!! DID YOU SEE THAT?!
WHAT'S THE BULBASAUR'S BEST ATTACK?!
FWP
EEP
NYONGG
OH, GREAT... WHAT NEXT?
WAIT... IF IT'S GOT A BULB...
CHOK!
HMM
MWAAA
BAM
WUP!
MMM...
TH-THERE'S NO WAY...
ARRG!!
!
GLINT
GLINT!!
WAIT...
WH-WHAT IF...? I GUESS I'VE GOTTA...

GLINT
BAM
...TRY THIS!!
Pff
SSSRROOOOO
M-MUHMUH--
MWOOOOMMM

YOU KNEW ABOUT THE BULBASAUR'S SOLARBEAM?
NAW... BUT I FIGURED, YOU KNOW, PLANTS TURN SUNLIGHT INTO ENERGY... AND THIS GUY HAS A PLANT ON ITS BACK...SO...
YOU JUST... FIGURED IT OUT?! AH-HA-HA-HA-HA-HA...
WA HAAA HAHAHA!!
?
THE BULBA-SAUR IS YOURS.
SEEMS HE'S TAKEN QUITE A LIKING TO YOU.
Y-YOU MEAN... REALLY? COOL!
BUT FIRST... I'VE GOTTA CLEAR SOMETHING UP. I DID NOT BREAK INTO YOUR POKÉ-MON LAB TO STEAL POKÉMON.
I ONLY WANTED YOU TO TEACH ME TO BE A BETTER POKÉMON TRAINER.
Y'SEE, YESTER-DAY—

HUH ?
BUT DO YOU KNOW WHAT IT TAKES TO BE GREAT?
...I SEE...
UHHH
...
IS THAT WHAT YOU THINK MAKES A GREAT POKÉMON TRAINER?
HAVING A POKÉMON POWER HOUSE IN YOUR ARSENAL?
KNOWING A LOT OF CLEVER TRICKS?
THAT FEELING FROM DEEP WITHIN... THAT'S THE KEY TO BECOMING A GREAT POKÉMON TRAINER.
THAT CONNECTION YOU HAD WITH THE BULBASAUR...
IF YOU DO... YOU'RE WRONG.
WHAT COUNTS IS WHAT'S *IN YOUR HEART!*

WHAT'S YOUR NAME, SON?
RED, SIR.
HERE, RED...
THIS IS A POKÉDEX... AN ENCYCLO-PEDIA OF POKÉMON.
WHENEVER YOU MEET AND LEARN ABOUT A NEW POKÉMON, ENTER YOUR DATA HERE.
PWIK
BY THE TIME YOU'VE INPUT THE DATA ON ALL THE POKÉMON...
...YOU MAY WELL HAVE BECOME ONE OF THE TRULY GREAT TRAINERS.
WOW! ME...
ONE OF THE GREATS...

RED! IF YOU EXPECT TO INPUT ANY VALUABLE DATA INTO THAT POKÉDEX, YOU CAN'T STAY HERE.
YOU HAVE TO *EXPAND* YOUR *TERRITORY*!
WHY NOT START WITH VIRIDIAN FOREST, NORTH OF THE CITY?
YOU'RE BOUND TO FIND POKÉMON THERE THAT YOU'VE NEVER SEEN BEFORE.
BESIDES, THAT HAPPENS TO BE WHERE...
AH-HA HA!
HA! NEVER MIND!
?
OOPS. I WAS IN SUCH A HURRY THAT...
I DIDN'T BRING VERY MANY POKÉ BALLS!
OH, WELL... THESE'LL HAVE TO DO...

I DON'T KNOW WHAT KIND OF POKÉMON WE'RE GONNA MEET...
BUT WITH POLIWHIRL AND BULBASAUR— WE'RE BOUND TO CATCH 'EM ALL!
KACH!
ALL RIGHTIE THEN!!
3 The Secret of Kangaskhan
LET'S GO!!
SHHH

THE VIRIDIAN FOREST
HSH
...
KACH!
CHAR-MANDER, GO!!
CHOOSH!
BON!
!
VNNN
MOMP!
...
SO... A VENO-MOTH...
FZZ
FZZ
FZZ

VENOMOTH
DATA
No. 049
DESCRIPTION: POISONMOTH
CATEGORIES: TYPE 1/BUG TYPE 2/POISON
HEIGHT: 4'11"
WEIGHT: 28.0 LB
ATTACKS: TACKLE, DISABLE, POISON POWDER, LEECH LIFE
◆The dustlike scales covering its wings are color coded to indicate the kinds of poison it has. It has a short life span and appears to be the evolved form of the Venonat.
PLIP
I'VE ALREADY CAUGHT ONE.
WILL YOU COME OUT...?
OH-HO-HO!
CHSH CHSH
STUPID CATER-PIE...
WHERE THE HECK DID IT GO?!
EE-YARRG!
CHSH
DID YOU CATCH IT?! DID YOU—
PLOGG
FWAK
GO, POLI-WHIRL!

FZZ
!!
WHAT ?!
FZZ
FZZ
SHHH~
SO THIS POLI-WHIRL HAS A TRAIN-ER...
GLAGG
POLI-WHIRL !
DON'T TAKE IT PERSON-ALLY.
WE THOUGHT IT WAS A WILD POKÉMON WHEN WE ATTACKED.
YOU DID THIS TO MY POLI-WHIRL— ?!
T.M.P
YOU'LL PAY !

WOK
RIDI-CU-LOUS!!
WE'RE BOTH IN THIS FOREST TO CAPTURE POKÉMON...
SO WE'RE BOUND TO CROSS PATHS SOMETIMES, AREN'T WE?
NN.
EH?
HEY...
YOU'RE...
YOU'RE *THAT GUY*!
WHY DO YOU KEEP...
BOOOOO-M
BOOOM
WH-WHAT'S *THAT*?
BOOM
AHHH... SO IT'S COME AT LAST...

BOOMMMM
KRAK
KAK
I HEARD YOU WERE AROUND HERE SOMEWHERE... BUT YOU'VE BEEN TESTING MY PATIENCE!
GAK!
EE-YAAAA!!
I'VE BEEN WAITING FOR YOU, KANGAS-KHAN!
KRAKLE
KRAAKLE
CHWOOOO
CHAR-MANDER, ATTACK!

I CAN'T WAIT TO ADD ITS DATA TO MY—
HEY! TH- THAT'S...
...A POKÉ- DEX ?!
MY GRANDDAD TOLD ME HE GAVE A POKÉDEX TO SOMEONE...
SO IT WAS YOU, HUH?
HA HA HA !!
A- HA HA HA HA!
GRRRR
WHAT'S SO FUNNY ?!
GR- GRAND- DAD? YOU MEAN...
...PRO- FESSOR OAK?!

THOUGH WHY HE'D GIVE A POKÉDEX TO THE LIKES OF YOU...
WELL, NEVER MIND! I'LL JUST SHOW YOU HOW IT'S DONE!
CHWOOO
CHAR-MANDER—FINAL BLOW!
CHOOOOSH!
GYAAAW !!
CHWOOOOOO
THAT SHOULD DO IT.
YOU'RE *MINE* !!
VSSH
!!
KANG
SHHH
O—OKAY, THEN! ONE MORE!
KANG

!
THE FIRE ATTACKS... NOT STRONG ENOUGH ?
CHSSSH
CHWOOOOOO
SOME-THING'S...
...WRONG...
CHWOOOOOO
IT'S STRONG ENOUGH TO REPEL THE POKÉ BALL... BUT IT ISN'T ATTACKING...
OF COURSE! THAT'S *IT*...
WAIT! STOP THE ATTACK !
NO WAY! THIS POKÉMON IS **MINE.** DON'T TRY TO STEAL IT FROM ME!
YOU DON'T UNDER-STAND! THE KANGA IS...
CHARMANDER—KEEP FIGHTING!
BUT...
CHWOOO

PLASH
CHA-PII!!
FWA
OH, JUST GET OUTTA MY WAY! POLIWHIRL!
HEY!! WHAT THE— WHAT'RE YOU-?!
WHERE DO YOU THINK YOU'RE GOING, YOU LITTLE-?!
VMM
ARE YOU OKAY?!
YOUR BABY... IS IT ALL RIGHT?!
EH?
WRGL
WRGL

POIK
IT'S HURT...
DID A POISON POKÉMON HURT YOU?
THERE— ALL BETTER NOW!
...
NO WONDER YOU WERE PROTECTING YOUR POUCH. IF THE FIRE HIT IT, YOUR SICK BABY COULD'VE GOTTEN BADLY HURT.
NNNG
BOOO--M

BOOOMM
HMPH. THANKS A **LOT**!
IF YOU HADN'T BUTTED IN, I COULD HAVE CAPTURED IT...
COME ON. YOU KNOW IT ISN'T REALLY WINNING...
...IF YOUR OPPONENT'S AT A DIS-ADVANTAGE.
FEH!
SAVE YOUR SLOGANS.
TMP TMP
H-HEY... WAIT UP!
MY NAME'S RED!
WHAT'S YOURS? HUH? HUH-?
WELL?!
!!
MY NAME'S **BLUE!!** NOW SHUT UP ALREADY AND LEAVE ME ALONE!!

BLUE... OKAY... !
HEY, BLUE! I'M NOT LOSING TO YOU!!
Y'HEAR ME, BLUE?! I'M GONNA WIN!
HA HA HA...
KSH
MY GRANDSON AND MY NEW PROTÉGÉ...
THE PATH TO BECOMING THE GREATEST POKÉMON TRAINER OF ALL HAS GOTTEN MORE COMPETITIVE.
GOOD LUCK TO YOU BOTH.

4 Wanted: Pikachu!
PEWTER CITY, IN THE WEST...
GET IT!
HURRY!
RUMBLE RUMBLE
THERE IT GOES!
RMMBLE!
RMBLE!
HUH?
WHIT
DMDMDM
FLUTTER
WANTED
PIKACHU
MISCHIEVOUS ELECTRIC MOUSE
REWARD FOR CAPTURE
PEWTER CITY MERCHANTS ASSOCIATION
PWAP!
SO THAT'S WHAT ALL THE FUSS IS ABOUT.
GUESS I'LL GIVE 'EM A HAND!

GRRN
THAT'S THE LAST TIME YOU'LL EAT MY PRODUCE!
WE'VE GOT YOU NOW, YOU PEST!
GRRMBL
GRRMBLL
HEY!
CH CH CH
DM DM DM
GET IT!!
VNN
NOW!
HSSSS
♪
CHUUU CHUUU

KLOMP
!
PIKU...
CHAK CHAK CHAK CHAK
#&@* !!!!
HEY! IT'S GETTING AWAY AGAIN!
ZOOM
UHHH
GET IT!!
DMDMDM
TSK... I CAN'T WATCH ANY MORE OF THIS.
OKAYYY...
POM

BULBASAUR—GO!
PO—NNN
BOM
MRGL
MRGL
PI ?!
MRGL MRGL
MRGL
A POKÉMON!
MRMRMRMR
GRRN
SNEEER
AUUGH!
CHAK

IT'S NO USE...
OH... MAN...
MRGL
MRGL
PI?!
BLIB!
BULBA-SAUR, ATTACK!
NOW IT'S ***OUR*** TURN.

POOF
?!
PADA
PADA
PADA
PIIIIIIIIII
...
HEH... PERFECT.
GFFF
START WITH SLEEP POWDER...
...THEN FINISH WITH...
...THIS!
PONNN
BOM
MRGL
GOTCHA!!
MRGL
MRGL
YAAAY!!
AND *THAT'S* HOW IT'S DONE!

YOUNG MAN, YOU'VE SAVED US!
THAT PEST WAS RUINING OUR BUSINESSES!
WE WISH YOU'D COME A LONG TIME AGO!
WHERE ARE YOU FROM?
I'M FROM PALLET TOWN.
BUT WHAT BROUGHT YOU *HERE?*
GLMP GLMP
WANNA KNOW?
THEN JUST WATCH WHILE I...
DO THIS!
PIK PIK
PIIP!
PIKACHU
DATA
No. 025
DESCRIPTION: MOUSE
CATEGORIES: TYPE 1/ ELECTRIC
HEIGHT: 1'04"
WEIGHT: 13.0 LB
ATTACKS: THUNDERSHOCK, THUNDER WAVE, QUICK ATTACK
When several of these Pokémon gather, their electricity could build and cause lightning storms. Forest dwellers, they are few in number and are exceptionally rare. The pouches on their cheeks discharge electricity at their opponents. The Pikachu are believed to be highly intelligent.

HMMM..
SO THIS WILD PIKACHU CAME OUT OF VIRIDIAN FOREST TO LIVE IN THE CITY...
WHAT AN AWESOME DEVICE!
IT WILL BE...
THERE ARE HUNDREDS OF POKÉMON IN THE WORLD...
ONCE I COLLECT ALL THEIR DATA... I'LL HAVE A COMPLETE POKÉDEX!
HUH?
GLMP
GLMP
HEY. COOL IT.
CHAKA CHAKA
WHAT'S WITH THIS THING?
WELL... OKAY THEN...

PIXX
PIXX
PIXX
WHOA !!
...
OKAY, PIKACHU... ?
HOW 'BOUT WE TRY TO BE FRIENDS?
COME ON! DON'T BE SO STUBBORN !
CHUUUU
CHAKK
AAAAGH !!
SHFF
GEEZ. YOU *LOOK* CUTE, BUT...
YOU'RE TAKING IT EASY ON THAT PIKACHU, AREN'T YOU, RED?

BLUE!
YOU'LL NEVER FILL YOUR POKÉDEX PLAYING AROUND LIKE THAT.
I'M EMBARRASSED TO HAVE YOU FOR A RIVAL ON THIS QUEST!
!!
RRRR
WHAT WAS THAT?!
SSSHHHH
A FIGHT, HUH?
KCH
GRRN
GRRN
KCH

BUT FIRST, MY IMPETUOUS FRIEND...
ALLOW ME TO LET YOU IN ON SOMETHING.
?
THIS TOWN'S GYM LEADER, BROCK, IS LOOKING FOR SOMEONE **WORTHY** TO FIGHT HIM.
I INTEND TO DO SO... AND WIN THE BOULDER BADGE.
THE "BOULDER BADGE"?
??
DON'T YOU KNOW?
THE BOULDER BADGE CAN BOOST THE ATTACK POWER OF YOUR POKÉMON.
EVERY POKÉMON TRAINER KNOWS THAT.
WELL, **SO-RRY**...
YOU #$@※!!

SO, HERE'S MY CHAL-LENGE TO YOU...
LET'S SEE WHICH OF US CAN WIN THE BOULDER BADGE FIRST.
OF COURSE, IT SHOULDN'T BE MUCH OF A MATCH SINCE YOU CAN'T EVEN TRAIN AN ELECTRIC MOUSE.
I'LL TAKE THAT CHALLENGE !
OH, AND ONE MORE THING.
PWIP
BROCK IS A ***ROCK*** POKÉMON TRAINER.
YOUR LITTLE ELECTRIC MOUSE WON'T BE ANY GOOD AGAINST HIM.
WELL, GOOD LUCK...
SHFFF
AND YOU'LL REGRET IT!
HA HA HA!

FWIP
...
WHAT A JERK...
CALLING ALL FIGHTERS!!
PEWTER CITY GYM LEADER BROCK WILL TAKE ON ALL CHALLENGERS!
DATES & TIMES:
CHALLENGER REQUIREMENTS:
PEWTER CITY:
GYM
SO THE NEXT CHALLENGE IS... TOMORROW AT NOON.
BLUE IS GONNA BE SORRY HE EVER—
LET'S *DO* IT!
WHOOPS. ALMOST FORGOT...
THE POKÉMON I BROUGHT WITH ME ARE LOW ON HEALTH.
FIRST THING IN THE MORNING, I NEED TO GO TO A POKÉMON CENTER...AND GET THESE GUYS HEALED!

NOTICE
OUR CENTER WAS DAMAGED YESTERDAY BY UNKNOWN VANDALS. WE WILL REOPEN WHEN OUR MACHINES ARE RUNNING AGAIN. WE APOLOGIZE FOR ANY INCONVENIENCE.
NEXT DAY AT THE POKÉMON CENTER...
GRMBL
GRMMBL
CENTER
KRASH KRASH
RRRGHHH
NO WAY...
KLANG KLANG KLANG
THAT MEANS...
PAKA
CHAKA
THE ONLY ONE I HAVE WHO'S AT FULL POWER IS... THIS ONE...

HUFF
HUFF
HUF
HUF
GYM
PEWTER CITY GYM
B.BAM
YAAAY! YAAAA!
FIGHT! FIGHT!
YAAAH! YAAY!
HWOOSH
YAAAAA
YAAAA
KILL! KILL!

5 Onix Is On!
IGHT!
BLUE !!
YAY! OOOOO
B-BROCK'S PRELIMINARY ROUND IS ABOUT TO START.
OOPS.
FWIP
FIGURES, WITH TH' PEWTER CITY GYM'S FINEST STANDIN' IN THE WAY.
I'VE SEEN MY SHARE O' FIGHTS HERE, BUT I'VE HARDLY EVER SEEN ANYBODY BLOW THROUGH THE PRELIMS TO GET TO BROCK.
MY NAME'S RED. NUMBER 18.
Reception Desk

COME ON, PUNK! LET'S GET THIS THING GOIN'!!
OH, GREAT...
IT'S HOPE-LESS.
PWI
OKAY! YOU'RE ON!!
WELL, I DON'T HAVE A CHOICE...
THEY'RE LOW ON HEALTH, BUT I'VE GOTTA FIGHT WITH THESE TWO.
BUT I COULDN'T TRAIN HIM!
HE'S THE ONLY ONE AT FULL HEALTH...
KLAAANG
...
THAT ONE DON'T LOOK LIKE MUCH TO ME!
DOES IT GOT ANY HEALTH LEFT, PUNK?

PLOSH!
LET'S WIN THIS WITH THE FIRST ATTACK, POLIWHIRL !!
!!
PLOB! PLOB! PLOB!
NOW— "ICE BEAM" !!
VVIRRRRRRRR
KA-KLING
AUGH!
PONN
WE CAN'T AFFORD TO TAKE EVEN ONE HIT OR— WE'RE FINISHED !!
HUF HUF

HE DOESN'T WASTE HIS ATTACKS EITHER. THE PUNK'S GOT STRATEGY!
HE'S ONLY GOT TWO O' THE THINGS, BUT WITH THE SWIFT WATER POKÉMON...
VVICHAH...
...AND THE POWER-FIGHTIN' GRASS POKÉMON, HE'S GOT GREAT BALANCE!
THAT KID SHOWED ME SOMETHIN'!
HE'S FINISHIN' EVERY FIGHT WITH HIS FIRST ATTACK.
YAAAAAY!
NOW HE FINALLY GETS TO FACE GYM LEADER BROCK!!
KRAK
HE DID IT AGAIN!!
AT LAST! AN OPPONENT WORTHY OF ME!

POLIWHIRL AND BULBASAUR ARE POOPED.
AT THE GYM'S BACK EN-TRANCE.
OH, C'MON, PIKACHU.
PWI!
OKAY?
JUST THIS ONE TIME... PLEASE!!
WELL... WE'RE UP.
ZH ZH ZH
NKH
KLAAAANG

SHHHHH
UH-OH!
PTU!
?!
...
WHERE'S YOUR FAMOUS FIRST ATTACK, BOY?!
GUESS I BETTER GO FIRST THEN!
DNN
DNNN-DNN
ROCK THROW!
CHWIP!
GONG!
GONG!
CHWIP!
BONG
CHWIP!
GONNNNG!
OH NO!
THE POKÉMON TOOK THE FULL BRUNT OF THE ATTACK!
LOOKS LIKE THIS IS THE END!
CHRRRR

PIK!
!!
CHAK CHAK CHAK CHAK
AA-AAA-RGH!!
?!
GASP!
OH!
WHAT A JOKE!
CHAK CHAK CHAK
WA HA HA HA!!!
MY ONIX'S ULTIMATE ATTACK IS... TO USE ITS *OWN BODY* AS A TORNADO!
THE SPEED OF ITS REVOLUTIONS SETS OFF *UNSTOPPABLE* SHOCK WAVES...
ONG ONG ONG ONG ONG ONG ONG ONG ONG
SO YOU WERE JUST WINNING WITH DUMB LUCK BEFORE!

CHAK
CHAK
CHAK
UHHH...
GRONNNG
GROONG
!
IT'S A BIG ONE! WATCH OUT, PIKACHU!
THE FINAL STRIKE...
..."SKULL BASH" !!
GROOOOOOOOO
GROOOOOO
!
GROO OO
GGONG!

SHHHHHHHH
YOU OKAY?
PI?!
WHEW... I'M GLAD...
LOOK, YOU DON'T HAVE TO FIGHT FOR ME IF YOU DON'T WANT TO.
I'M SORRY I FORCED YOU INTO THIS.
HOW 'BOUT WE JUST TRY TO BE FRIENDS?
FEH. WE WON'T MISS THIS TIME!
RRRRR
ONIX-ATTACK!
GROOOOO

CHZ
CHZ
CHZ
PI
OOOOOONNN
CHWRRRR
CHAK
CHAK
CHAK
CHZZ CHZZ CHZZ CHZZ
CHZZ CHZZ CHZ
CHAK CHAK CHAK
BLASH
WHAT—?!

KRAAAASH
NOOOO !!
GONK
IT...IT CAN'T BE.
SHHHHH
WH-WHAT'S... ?
WHAT'S... HAP-PENING... ?
WHOA!
...
TA
HOO-RAAAAAAAY!
...

SO BLUE AND I ENDED UP BEING THE ONLY ONES TO WIN THE BOULDER BADGE.
...
THANKS, PIKACHU.
I COULDN'T HAVE DONE IT WITHOUT YOU.
MEET POLIWHIRL AND BULBASAUR.
THEY'RE GOOD FRIENDS OF MINE.
WE'D LOVE TO HAVE YOU JOIN US... IF YOU WANT TO!

SHAKE ON IT...?
CHUUUU
PIK!
?
CHAK
CHAK
CHAK
EE-AAARGH!!
WHAT WAS *THAT* FOR?!
AND JUST WHEN I THOUGHT I WAS FINALLY GETTING SOME-WHERE...!!
CHZ
CHZ
CHZ

HHYUUUUUUUUUUUU
GRRN
DRRP
hff
hff
GYAOOOOOOO
GASP!
IT'S THE HYDRO PUMP! STARYU, GET AWAY!!
DOOOOSSSS

GLAAASSSHHH
!!
6 Gyarados Splashes In!
WHY, YOU...
STAR-YU !!
PLASH
GYIII
RIIII...
PLASH

TAKING ON A PRETTY BIG ONE, AREN'T YOU?
!
ZK
LET ME HELP.
ZZZMMM
STAY BACK, YOU! THIS IS DANGEROUS!
HEH HEH.
I'LL BE FINE! I'M NOT JUST ANY KID!
AND BY THE WAY—THE NAME'S NOT "YOU"!
KCH
SPECIFICALLY... IT'S "RED"!
OKAY, BULBASAUR... GO!
BON!

...
WATCH IT! IT'S THE HYDRO PUMP!
GYORRAA
A POKÉMON!
YOU'RE A POKÉMON TRAINER TOO?
DOOOOOOOSSSSS!
HEH... NO WATER ATTACK'S GONNA WORK ON A GRASS POKÉMON!
HUH...?
IZZAT POKÉMON SMILING...?
WHOA!
PLASH PLASH

NOW IT'S OUR TURN!
BULBASAUR... ATTACK!!
BLP!
BSH!
SRRRRRRRR
GNNGGNNG
GWAAAR?!
KKKKKK!
LEECH SEED?
YOU GOT IT!
NOW'S OUR CHANCE! RECOVER!

RYUUUUUUUUUUUP!
OKAY, STARYU... YOUR INJURIES ARE HEALED!
HEY... NOW *THAT* IS A SWEET TRICK!
GYAAAWRRR!!
GRRN
BWIK BWIK
SHOULD WE START DOUBLE-DATING!
WE SHOULD!
BULBA-SAUR!!
STARYU!!

RRUUP
BUBBLE-
BEAM
!
SHHH
VINE
WHIP
!
RRUUP
!!
BOM
MRRGL
MRRGL
MRRGL
AND LAST
BUT NOT
LEAST... THE
POKéBALL!
GYAWAAAA
MRRGL
MRRGL
SHHHHHHH
POOOM

GOT HIM!
...
PHEW!!
THOMP
TH-THANKS A LOT... UMM...UHH...
ONE MORE TIME—THE NAME'S RED!
I DIDN'T EXPECT TO SEE A POKÉMON THAT BIG... NOT HERE OF ALL PLACES!
WAS IT WILD OR WAS IT...?
GYARADOS IS A WATER POKÉMON. AND IT'S NOT SUPPOSED TO LIVE IN HABITATS LIKE THIS...
I FIGURED. SO... WHAT'S IT DOING HERE?
THAT GYARADOS ISN'T WILD.
IT'S MY POKÉMON.
WHAAAAT?!!
PAP PAP
PAP PAP
I WAS RAISING IT... 'TIL LAST WEEK, WHEN SOMEBODY STOLE IT.
WHEN IT CAME BACK... IT WASN'T THE SWEET GYARADOS I KNEW ANY-MORE...

I'VE BEEN TRACKING IT... NOT HARD TO DO SINCE IT'S BEEN DESTROYING EVERYTHING IN ITS PATH...
ANYWAY, THANKS FOR THE HELP. EVERYTHING'S OKAY N—
IT IS NOT!
...
IT'S NEVER OKAY WHEN A POKÉMON GOES BERSERK!
THOSE GUYS WHO STOLE GYARADOS MUST BE RESPONSIBLE FOR THIS!
I'M GOING TO GO KICK THEIR BUTTS!
WHERE DO YOU THINK YOU'RE GOING?
WHERE?! I'M... UH...
THOSE THIEVES... YOU SAID THEY WERE...
...WHERE'D YOU SAY THEY WERE?
Listen...
IF I KNEW, DON'T YOU THINK I'D BE THERE?!

?
MM
HEY! MAYBE THE PROF. KNOWS SOME-THING...
POKÉ-MON CEN-TER
POKE CENTER
PIK PIK PIK
AW, SHUCKS!
THAT'S PROFESSOR OAK. HE'S THE WORLD'S LEADING EXPERT ON POKÉMON.
PING
OHO, RED!
IT'S BEEN A WHILE!
GETTING CLOSER TO COMPLETING YOUR POKÉDEX, RED?
'SMATTER OF FACT, I AM! I EVEN GOT SOME NEW DATA TODAY! TAKE A LOOK...
VWIP
THERE ARE HUNDREDS OF VARIETIES OF POKÉMON...
...SCATTERED ALL OVER THE EARTH.

OHOHO... GYARADOS...
A POKÉDEX?
GYARADOS
DATA
No. 130
DESCRIPTION: ATROCIOUS
CATEGORIES: TYPE 1/WATER TYPE 2/FLYING
HEIGHT: 21' 04"
WEIGHT: 518.0 LB
ATTACKS: DRAGON RAGE, BITE, HYDRO PUMP
The evolved form of Magikarp. Rarely seen in the wild. Huge and vicious, it is capable of destroying entire cities in a rage. Can fire a Hyper Beam from its mouth.
IT'S A HIGH-TECH ENCYCLO-PEDIA.
TO INPUT ALL THE DATA...ON ALL THE POKÉMON...
THAT'S MY GOAL IN LIFE!
BLAH BLAH BLAH
AH, YES... EVOLVING FROM A MAGIKARP, IT...
...HYDRO PUMP...
WHENEVER I CATCH A POKÉMON, ITS DATA AUTOMATICALLY GETS INPUTTED.
WEREN'T YOU PAYING ATTENTION?!
OH, I ALMOST FORGOT! HEY, PROF! I HAVE A QUESTION!
...THUS, CLEARLY...
KWIP!
YEAH!
I'LL HAVE TO FIGHT WILD POKÉMON AND TOUGH TRAINERS ON THE WAY...
BUT I'LL BE A TOP POKÉMON TRAINER MYSELF ONE O' THESE...

MM-HM... SO THE POKÉMON REFUSES TO LISTEN TO ITS TRAINER... AFTER JUST A FEW DAYS...
SOUNDS LIKE THE DOINGS OF TEAM ROCKET!
TEAM ROCKET ?!
TEAM ROCKET! A SECRET SOCIETY THAT USES POKÉMON FOR EVIL!
RECENTLY, THEY'RE RUMORED TO BE CONDUCTING LAB EXPERIMENTS ON POKÉMON...
USING POKÉ-MON...
...FOR LAB EXPERI-MENTS... !!
DISTRESSING, I KNOW. BUT THERE IS SOMETHING YOU CAN DO TO HELP. ON MOUNT MOON, JUST TO YOUR EAST, THERE IS REPUTED TO BE A MOON STONE.
WHAT'S THAT... ?
A STONE, THEY SAY, THAT IS ABLE TO BOOST THE POWER OF A POKÉMON... ENORMOUSLY !
IT'S LIKELY THAT TEAM ROCKET IS AFTER THIS STONE...
...
...

THAT DOES IT!
I CAN'T WAIT TO COMPLETE THE POKÉDEX, BUT...
...FIRST I'M GONNA FIND THESE TEAM ROCKET GUYS...
AND I'M GONNA KICK... THEIR...
...
WHAT?
I'M GOING WITH YOU!
HUH?!
MOUNT MOON IS ON THE WAY TO MY HOME-TOWN...
IF I GO WITH YOU, I'M BOUND TO RUN INTO A LOT OF TRAINERS I KNOW.
I MIGHT BE ABLE TO GET MORE INFOR-MATION ON THIS TEAM ROCKET!
WAIT A MINUTE! Y-YOU DON'T THINK *YOU* CAN TAKE ON...
KCHK
SSHHH

I FORGOT TO INTRODUCE MYSELF. MY NAME'S MISTY.
I'M FROM CERULEAN CITY. NICE TO MEET YOU!
I'M A WATER POKéMON TRAINER.
THE CAVES IN THE MOUNTAIN ARE FULL OF ROCK POKéMON...
I THINK I CAN HOLD MY OWN JUST FINE. ♡
...
SHP
UH...
UHHH
OKAY, THEN! WE'RE OFF!
FULL SPEED AHEAD!

7 Raging Rhydon

WHOA!!
SOMEBODY'S THERE!!
GOOSH
IS THAT TEAM ROCKET?
I THINK SO...
THOSE JERKS ARE EVERYWHERE...
WAIT A MINUTE... THAT UNIFORM...
QUICK—INTO THE CAVES.
KSSH KSSH
YOU THINK I'M GONNA BACK DOWN NOW?!
SO WHAT NOW?
EXACTLY WHAT WE NEED.
SOMEWHERE IN THERE IS A MOON STONE THAT CAN BOOST A POKÉMON'S POWER.

DEEP IN THE CAV- ERNS...
IT'S AWFUL DARK...
FWSSH
PLIP
PLIP
GRAB
HEH HEH... JUST LEAVE EVERY- THING TO ME!
'KAY, BRIGHT EYES—I'M COUNTIN' ON YOU!
POM
IS THAT A... PIKACHU ?
AIN'T MICKEY MOUSE.
DOESN'T EXACTLY LOOK THRILLED TO BE HERE...
PCHH!
CHZZ CHZZ
YEAH. LIFE'S TOUGH, LITTLE FELLA...
CHZZZ CHZZ
CHZZZ CHZZ
CHZZZ CHZZ
BUT PIKACHU'S ONE TALENTED LITTLE–
CHUUUUU
AWP.
LIGHT'S ON!
FWISH
PLIP
PLIP

TONK
YUURRG !!
HUH ?
RED... LOOK UP...
STUPID ROCK! I OUGHTTA...
RRRR
AAAAAAA !!!
POP
WELL. IF IT ISN'T TOM SAWYER AND LITTLE BECKY IN THE CAVE.
HEH!

AND WHO ARE *YOU?*
SNORT!
YOU'RE TEAM ROCKET!!
YOU KNOW US. WE'RE FLATTERED.
CHHH
LET'S *DO* IT!!
LET ME ANSWER YOU LIKE THIS...
I *CHALLENGE YOU!!*
HNN
HNN
PI!
PIKA-CHU!!
HNN
HNN
RHH
RHH
RHYHORN! ROCK BLAST!
RHH

KLAK!
CHX
CHX
CHX
SHHHHHHH
CHXX...
CHXX...
CHXX...
CHXX
CHXX
CH
CH
CH
CHXX...
P-KYUUUU
PWIIIII
FWEE
CHOM
@#
!!
CHAX
CHAX
CHAX
YOU MAY *LOOK* CUTE, PIKACHU– BUT *OOH*, YOU SURE ARE *ORNERY* !!

HEHH
AH. TAKES ME BACK TO WHEN I WAS A BOY.
CHZ CHZ
LET ME GIVE YOU A LITTLE TASTE OF... REALITY.
?!
CRUSH THEM!!
GNSH
RREEE!
DN
DN
DN
RAAR

ARE YOU RESPONSIBLE FOR WHAT HAPPENED TO MY GYARADOS?!
...
HE TURNED RHYHORN... INTO RHYDON... !!
YOU...
...ROT-TEN...
YOU THINK WE REMEMBER EVERY LITTLE POKÉMON WE EXPERIMENT ON?
HOW SHOULD WE KNOW?
SHYUUU
STARYU! ATTACK!!
BOM
DEAR ME... DO YOU THINK SO?
SHB SHB SHB SHB
WE GOT 'EM!!
IT'S WORKIN' !!

HORN DRILL !!
?!
RRRN!
DDDDD DDDDD DDDDD
RUUU
AUGH!
WAK
GLAG
SHHH
YEEE

DOMP
Ugh!
KUNK
MISTY
!
THEY'LL
PAY
FOR
THIS!
PERHAPS...
IN SOME OTHER
LIFETIME.
OH,
YEAH
?!
PIKA-
CHU,
AT-
TACK
!
RRRR CHUUUU
!

RRREEEEE
RHYDON, ATTACK!
IT'S OVER!
DOOOM
DN DN DN
RRD
CHH CHH
DNK
DNK
DNK
I GUESS NOBODY WINS *EVERY* FIGHT... BUT I'M NOT GONNA LOSE...
...TO JERKS LIKE *YOU!*
CHH CHH CHH CH CH
CHH CHH
PIKACHU... NOW!!

CHAXX X
DONNNNNG
CHCH CH CHCH
WHERE ARE YOU FLYING, PIKACHU? OUT OF CONTROL, PERHAPS...?!
CHX CHX
CH CH CH
?
CHCH CH CH CHCHCH CH

GRRRMMMMMMM
SHH
SHHH
Z-BOOOOOOM
GONE!
THEY'RE GONE!

POW
HAI-YAH
DNG!
YOU GOT ME ALL DIRTY!
HUH?
WHAT THE—?! I'M COVERED IN DIRT!!
HUFF
HUF
OHHH... WHERE AM I?
MT. MOON EXIT

SURE... WHAT-EVER...
I NAILED RHYDON WITH PIKACHU IN ONE SHOT AN' THEN I...
YOU SHOULDA SEEN ME IN THERE!
HEY, IF YOU'D LET ME FINISH MY STORY...
BUT WE DIDN'T GET THE MOON STONE AND—
THE CAVE COLLAPSED... AND THERE IT WAS!
SHHH
EEP !!
TA-DAAA!
YOU DID IT!
NOW LET'S USE IT!

CERULEAN CITY— THE CITY OF WATER ...
THIS IS A JOKE, RIGHT?
8 Suddenly Starmie
I MEAN THIS PLACE...
THERE'S NO WAY THIS IS YOUR HOUSE!
'FRAID SO.
THE NAME'S RED.
YO.
I'D LIKE YOU TO MEET SOME-BODY...
Y-YOUR LADYSHIP IS...IS DIRTY!
WEL-COME HOME, LADY MISTY.
PITA!
PITA!
PITA!

TINK
TINK TINK
FLAP
FLAP
FLAP
WOW! I COULD GET USED TO THIS!
SORRY TO KEEP YOU WAITING!
WHOA! YOU DIDN'T TELL ME THIS WAS A COSTUME PARTY!
OH, SHUT UP.
JUST EAT YOUR DINNER.

...
'COURSE, IT ONLY TOOK ME A FEW MINUTES TO MOP THEM UP!
KLNK
...AND THEN MISTY GOT KNOCKED OUT! SO IT WAS ME AGAINST ALL OF TEAM ROCKET!
K-TINK!
K-TANK!
HEY, RED.
THERE'S SOMETHING I GOTTA TALK TO YOU ABOUT...
WHAT IS IT, MISTY? CAN'T STAND LISTENING TO HOW I SAVED THE DAY WHILE YOU WERE SNOOZING?
SHUT UP. LISTEN, OUR POKéMON WILL BE FULLY HEALED SOON.
WHEN THEY ARE, I THINK WE NEED TO PUT 'EM ON A SERIOUS TRAINING REGIMEN.
MAX
MIN
TRAIN-ING...?
YUP. THOSE DOPES WE FOUGHT AT MT. MOON CAN'T BE THE BEST TEAM ROCKET'S GOT.
WE'RE GOING TO HAVE MORE OPPONENTS TO FACE. BETTER ONES. STRONGER ONES.

GOONS LIKE THAT MIGHT SCARE YOU, BUT I KNOW HOW TO HANDLE 'EM!
WHAT...?!
AHH, CHILL OUT.
D'YOU WANT TO GET YOUR STUPID SELF HURT?!
YOU IDIOT!!
YOU WOULDN'T SAY THAT...
...IF YOU HADN'T SLEPT THROUGH MY PERFORMANCE!
!
...
BAM
SHEESH. YOU DON'T HAVE TO TAKE IT PERSONALLY!

DID I SAY SOME-THING WRONG ?
NAH... ANYWAY, WHO'S GOT TIME FOR TRAINING?
THERE'S A WHOLE MANSION FULL OF CUTE MAIDS FOR ME TO ASK OUT!
PFF
?!
HYUUUU
HEY, WHAT'S WITH THIS WIND ?!
WAAAGGA!
AIEE
SOME-BODY HELP MEEEE...
POM
PWING
SHWRR

WHOOSH
WHOOOSH
fffp
...
SHHHHHHH
...
PLIK
I-IT'S OVER...?
HUHH HUH
WAIT... WHAT'S THIS... ?
A SCALE...! A GYARADOS SCALE!

tweeee
tweeee
...
HMMM
IS SOMEBODY AFTER ME...?
UM... MR. RED?
PL- PLEASE EXCUSE US, BUT...
HUH?
OH, I GET IT. YOU WANNA SEE ME IN ACTION?
OH, YES, SIR!
WELL, IF YOU *INSIST*... I CAN GIVE YOU A LITTLE SAMPLE THIS VERY DAY!
OH, BUT HOW?
CERULEAN CITY MUST HAVE A *GYM LEADER*, RIGHT?
JUST FOR YOU— I'M GONNA CHALLENGE HIM AND KICK HIS BUTT!

Tee hee hee
WHAT'RE YOU LAUGHIN' ABOUT? YOU DON'T THINK I *CAN*?!
Tee Hee Hee
N-NO, SIR... IT'S JUST THAT...
AHEM SO YOU WANT TO FIGHT THE CERULEAN CITY GYM LEADER, DO YOU?
THEN COME WITH ME.
I'LL TAKE YOU THERE MYSELF.
HEY, WAIT UP! HOW FAR IS THIS GYM?
HEY!!
IT'S AT THE EDGE OF THE CITY.
NOT VERY CONVEN-IENT...

GYM CERULEAN CITY
VOILA!
PLEASE...
AFTER YOU.
KRIII
HEH HEH HEH
?
SHHHHHHH
KRIK
KRIK
DON'T TELL ME THE IDIOT ISN'T HERE!
WE'VE CHECKED ALL THE ROOMS!
HWOOOO
WHERE IS THIS MORON GYM LEADER, ANYWAY?!
THE MOR-ON...

...IS RIGHT HERE!
?!
HA! HA! HA! HA!
OKAY, YEAH. I GET IT. FUNNY.
NOW WHERE IS HE REALLY?
BLASSHH!
GWAHH!!
WHAT TH...?
TOOM TOOM
N-NOW HOLD ON A SECOND... LET'S—
SWSSHH
...

SHTOM
WAK!
STM STM STM
EEP
EEP
EEP
NOT IN A FIGHTING MOOD? WHAT IF I TOLD YOU...
...THE ONE WHO ATTACKED YOU LAST NIGHT... WAS *ME*?!
SKWISH-
NO WAY!
STM
GLUG
WELL, IF YOU SAY SO...
RRRRR
YOU'LL REGRET THAT!
BOM
BULBASAUR!!

BWNN!
VINE WHIP !!
A VINE WHIP...?
SPAP
YOU GOTTA BE KID-DING.
BUBBLE-BEAM !!
SHAA
GLOG
MEEBLE! MEEBLE!
WH-WHAT'S GOTTEN INTO YOU, ANYWAY...?
...
I THOUGHT... Y-YOU KNEW HOW I FELT...

...ABOUT US AS A TEAM...
...
I JUST KNOCKED YOU DOWN, BUT... STARMIE WASN'T ENOUGH AT MT. MOON...
DON'T YOU GET IT?! WE HAVE TO GET REAL OR THEY'LL FLATTEN US!
WE HAVE TO BE AT OUR BEST! AND WE HAVE TO WORK TOGETHER!!
SHE DID ALL THIS JUST TO PROVE...?
YOU'RE RIGHT.
I DON'T HAVE TIME TO IMPRESS GIRLS.
AND YOU DON'T HAVE TIME FOR TEARS!
!
LET'S GO TRAIN!

WE'VE LEARNED EACH OTHER'S SKILLS AND ATTACKS.
YUP.
NOW IT'S TIME TO HONE THOSE SKILLS ON OUR OWN.
ARE YOU CERTAIN IT'S WISE TO LET HIM GO?
A FEW DAYS LATER..
BUT I DO LOOK FORWARD...
...TO MEETING HIM AGAIN.
SEE YA, MISTY!

NOT FAR FROM CERULEAN CITY...
DANG IT! THE THANG'S GONE KABLOOIE AGAIN!
THIS HERE POKÉMON TRANSPORTER DON'T RUN NO BETTER'N A METAPOD IN MOLASSES!
FIXIN' IT'S JES' ONE BIG OL' PAIN IN THE–
KREEEEEEE
TUGG
BLANG!
OH, DOUBLE-DANG !!
KLIK
AUTO TIMER
VREEE-EEE-EE-EEEE
BAM
BAMM
BAM

9 ...But Fearow Itself!
ROUTES 24-24
RRGH GOT SO MANY POKÉ BALLS I CAN'T CARRY 'EM ALL...
B-BONK
BUT I WORKED SO HARD TO CATCH 'EM ALL, I CAN'T JUST LEAVE 'EM BEHIND BECAUSE THEY'RE...
...SO... HEAVY...
HUH ?!
ZZZZZ...
THAT'S A RATTATA... I THINK.
BUT SOME-THIN'S NOT RIGHT ABOUT IT...
ZZZZZ

CREEP!
IT'S GOTTA BE A NEW KIND OF POKÉMON!! AW-RIGHT!!
HOO-WEE! WHO'D'A THUNK IT'D BE SO HARD JES' TO LIGHT A *FIRE*?
HECK, IF I WAS HUMAN AH C'D PICK THIS OL' STICK UP JES' LAK IT WAS A...A STICK!
HUH ?
A P-POKÉMON THAT...
...TALKS ?!
EEEYAH!
!
HOT DANG! A HUMAN BEAN!
AH WAS STARTIN' T'THINK NOBODY'D EVER COME MOSEYIN' OUT HYAR!
UH...UH...
BUT PRAISE BE! C'MON, YOUNG FELLA, LEND ME A HAND!
...
B-B-BUT-
WHAT IS IT, BOY? SUMP'N SCARE YA?

FRRRR!
NAME'S BILL, AN' THIS HERE'S SEA COTTA–
FWINK
AHEM!
WULL, AH MAY **LOOK** LIKE JES' A MUTATED RATTATA... BUT AH'LL HAVE YEW KNOW I'M A POKÉMON EXPERT!
ROOSH!
R– RIGHT...
NOD
NOD
VIP
NOD
H... H... HELP... ?
WULL, DON' JES' **STAN'** THERE, BOY!
HELLLLP!
HEY, WAIT **UP**!

FWIP
♫
BNNNNNNNNN
WHAT KINDA LAME ATTACK IS THAT!?
SWRRRR R
BULBASAUR— RAZOR LEAF!
FIRST I GOTTA STOP THE FEAROW!
WHADDYA THINK SOME GRASS POKÉMON'S GONNA DO FOR YA?!
hmph
NOW LISTEN, BOY!
IF'N YOU WANNA STOP A FLYIN' POKÉMON, FIRST THANG Y' DO IS PARALYZE ITS WANGS!
HRG
IF IT'LL SHUT YOU UP...
Y'GOT TWO YOU C'N USE! USE 'EM!
WRRR
CHUUM
PIKACHU— THUNDER WAVE!
POLIWHIRL— ICE BEAM!

CHAK CHAK CHAK
FWIP
CH
CHH
EEEE-OOOO!!
OOPS...
WHAT'RE YOU SHOOTIN' AT ME FER?!
Y'AIMIN' T'FRY ME?!
DON'T EVEN TRY WHILE TH' DANG THANG'S FLYIN'!
JES' WAIT 'TIL IT STOPS!
YOU THINK I CAN KEEP UP WITH...
WAIT!
RRMBL
RRMMBBL

PIII!
PIKA-CHU !!
CHMMMMM
!
RRMMBBL
RRMBL
RRMBL
WHAT ?!
CHH CHH CH CHH
RRRM...
RRM-RRMM
IF YOU MISS FROM BELOW-TRY FROM ABOVE !
Y' DO WANNA FRY ME!
YEEEEEE

GOTCHA !!
HYOOOO
AAAAA !!
CHOOOOM
!!
OMP!
FRRR
WHOA-HO.
CHZ
CHZ
FWIK
SO... NOT A LOT OF FIGHT IN YOU **NOW**, EH?
TUP

ROOSH!
AUGH!!
OHHHH...
OWWWW...
UH... I KNOW THAT STANCE...
ROO--
HEY, BOY!!
BETTER WATCH OUT—

FROOOO
--FER TH'DRILL PECK!!
HUH?
FROOOO
POK
!!

PSSHHHHHH
...
!!
P... PP...
WOOOOOOOOO
?!

FONK
WHEW !!
PWIP PWIP PWIP
ANY TIME, BOY... ANY TIME...
THANKS !!
IT HELPED TO KNOW WHAT ATTACK WAS COMING NEXT!
DON'T TELL ME YA *PLANNED* THAT...

BWEEEEN
1
2
K-CHIK!
SEA COTTAGE...

FSSHHHH
HOT DIGGETY DAWG!
NO CHANCE AH COULDA GOT BACK TO NORMAL BY M'SELF! MUCH OBLIGED, BOY!
WHAT *IS* THIS THING?
A POKÉMON TRANS-PORTER!
THIS HERE CONTRAPTION'LL TRANSPORT POKÉMON... OR WHUTEVER Y'WANT... ANYWHERE Y'WANT IT!
THAT IS SO *COOL*!
STILL GOT A FEW BUGS T'WORK OUT, THOUGH...
HMMM
LIKE IF YA GOT A RATTATA IN *ONE* CYLINDER AN' IT STOPS WORKIN' AN' THEN YA FALL INTO THE *OTHER* CYLINDER AN'...
...
WELL, YA GET THE PITCHER. LIKE AH SAID...
...TH' NAME'S BILL.
I'M RED.
AND I'M ON A MISSION... TO BECOME THE GREATEST POKÉMON TRAINER WHO EVER LIVED!

A BOY WITH A MISSION! THAT'S WHUT AH LIKE TO SEE!
TELL YA WHUT, BOY! AH'M GONNA HELP YOU! AH AIN'T A POKÉMON EXPERT FER NOTHIN', Y'KNOW!
WE GOTTA LIGHTEN YER LOAD!
AH'LL TAKE THESE!
FWIP!
HEY-!
NOW, NOW! WITH MY TRANSPORTER AH CAN SHOOT THESE TO YA INSTANTLY, WHEREVER YA HAPPEN TA-
HUH?
YOW!!
F... FEAROW!!

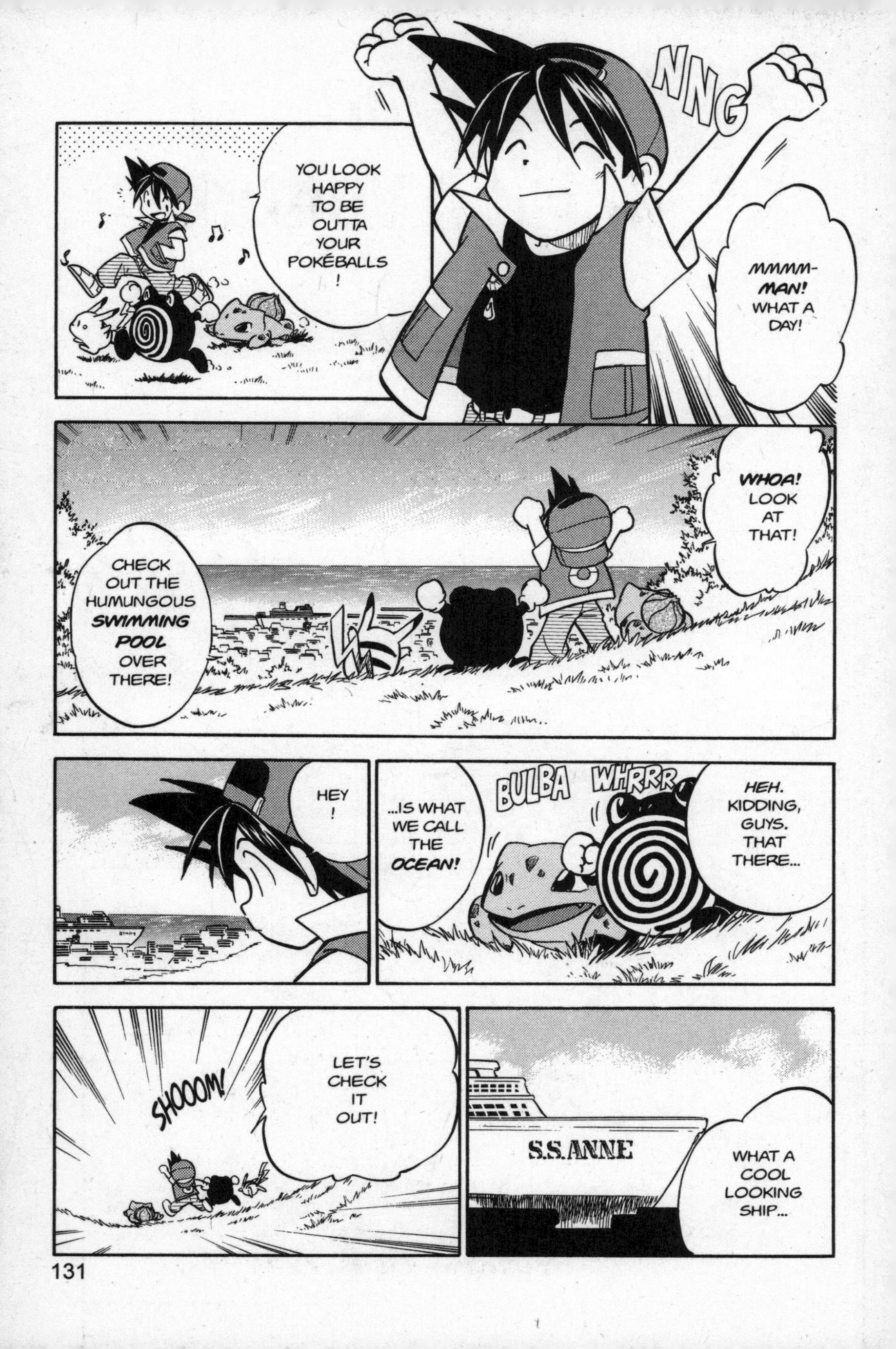
NNG
MMMM-MAN! WHAT A DAY!
YOU LOOK HAPPY TO BE OUTTA YOUR POKÉBALLS!
WHOA! LOOK AT THAT!
CHECK OUT THE HUMUNGOUS SWIMMING POOL OVER THERE!
HEH. KIDDING, GUYS. THAT THERE...
...IS WHAT WE CALL THE OCEAN!
BULBA
WHRRR
HEY!
WHAT A COOL LOOKING SHIP...
S.S.ANNE
LET'S CHECK IT OUT!
SHOOOM!

10 Danger: High Voltorb

I CAN'T BELIEVE I'M GETTING AWAY WITH THIS!
I WONDER HOW FAR I CAN GO!
RATTTTLE
RATTTTLE
RATTTTLE
DID I JUST... HEAR SOME-THING...?
I MUST BE GET-TING JUMPY!
RATTTLE
RATTTLE
HMMM.
I COULD USE A MAP...
KRIII
KRIII
GLINT
ULP?
WH-WH-WHAT WAS THAT...?
MMZ...

GET HIM !!
A STOW-AWAY !
!
BMM
BMM BMM
MWOB!
YAAA !!
S.S. ANNE
DIDN'T HAVE TO GET SO ROUGH...
DONG
AND STAY OUT!
OUCH !!
HMMM
WAIT A SEC... THAT THING... IT HAD TO BE A POKÉMON.
BUT WHAT'S IT DOING ON A SHIP... ?
!!
HUH?
TAP
YOUNG MAN...
? ? ?

THOSE SPHERES YOU'RE WEARING...
MIGHT THOSE BE, BY ANY CHANCE... POKÉ BALLS?
Y-YEAH. WHO ARE–?
GOOD FOR YOU, MY BOY! SO YOUNG BUT ALREADY A POKÉMON TRAINER!
IS THAT SO AMAZING?
AH! AND HUMBLE BESIDES!
I CAN SEE YOU'RE NOT JUST ANY LAD!
NOW, LET'S HAVE A LOOK AT WHAT'S IN THOSE POKÉ BALLS, EH?!
B-B-BUT THEY'RE...
GOMP
SHOW ME! SHOW ME!
BOM
BOM
BOM
CUT IT *OUT*!
RE-MARK-ABLE!!
SIMPLY REMARK-ABLE!
YOU'RE *IN*!
YOU, MY LAD, ARE NOW AN HONORARY MEMBER OF THE ***POKÉMON FAN CLUB!***
"POKÉMON... FAN... CLUB"...?

IN VERMILION CITY...
POKÉMON FAN CLUB
WE LOVE POKÉMON
DON'T BE SHY, SON!
BAMM!
YOU THERE, MY GIRL?
WILL YOU TAKE THIS TO THE POST OFFICE?
A POKÉ-MON STAMP?!
I SWEAR, THERE'S NOTHING MORE GOLDARN STUBBORN THAN A CATERPIE! HEH-HEH!
WELL, AT LEAST THEY DON'T HAVE HAIR-BALLS...LIKE MY RATTATA! TEE-HEE!
LAD, YOU'LL NEVER FIND A MORE DEVOTED GAGGLE OF POKÉMON LOVERS THAN IN THIS ROOM!
Y-YEAH?
TAKE A LOOK!
THE NEWS-LETTER SAYS IT ALL!
ポケモンクラブ会報
WE ♡ POKÉMON
A CASE OF POKÉ-LOVE
That's the last bath I'll take with my Tentacool."
A BATH WITH A...?

EVERYONE, PLEASE! MAY I HAVE YOUR ATTENTION?
ALLOW ME TO INTRODUCE OUR NEWEST MEMBER... MY FRIEND RED!
W-WHOA... WAIT... I... I...
OOH
AAAH
GOLLY !!
THESE POKÉMON ARE CERTAINLY USED TO PEOPLE, AREN'T THEY?
RUBB
RUBB
AREN'T THEY CUTE!
HOW LONG HAVE YOU HAD THIS POLIWHIRL?
SINCE I WAS A KID...
WHOOOSHH
...AND POLIWHIRL WAS JUST A POLIWAG!
GOOD-NESS !
THEY *ARE* WELL BEHAVED, AREN'T THEY?!
WELL, WE'VE BEEN TRAV-ELING TO-GETHER FOR A LONG TIME!
AND THEY'VE BAILED ME OUT OF PLENTY OF BATTLES!

HUSSSSSSSHHH
?!
YOU MAKE YOUR POKÉMON... DO BATTLE?
WH-WHAT ELSE WOULD I DO WITH THEM?
WHAT KIND OF POKÉMON LOVERS WOULD WE BE IF WE MADE THEM FIGHT?!
THEY HAVE TO FIGHT TO EVOLVE!!
POKÉMON FAN CLUB
WE LOVE POKÉMON
OURS JUST STAY LITTLE AND CUTE FOREVER!
TEE HEE
FOMP
...
HELLLLP!!
BAMM!
SOME-ONE STOLE MY EXEG-GUTOR!!
GASP...
NOT... AGAIN...
SNIF

WHAT'S WRONG?
THE DIRECTOR'S ABRA WAS STOLEN LAST MONTH!
IT'S HAPPENING TO ALL OF US.
THAT'S A LOT OF POKÉMON.
AND THERE'S... NOTHING... WE CAN... CAN...
SOBB...
BWA-AAAA!!
BOOO HOO
A POKÉ-NAPPER, EH...?
BAMM
TELL ME EVERYTHING YOU KNOW ABOUT THIS CASE!

HMMM
MEANING THE THIEVES WOULD HAVE TO BE ABLE TO TRANSPORT FULL-SIZED POKÉMON SOMEHOW...
BUT IT'D BE TOO HARD FOR ANYBODY BUT THE OWNERS TO GET THE POKÉMON INTO THEIR POKÉ BALLS...
SO THE ABDUCTIONS HAPPEN AROUND THE SAME TIME EVERY MONTH.
YES.
OKAY...
D'YOU KNOW WHERE THAT SHIP IS HEADED?
I'VE HEARD THAT LT. SURGE, THE VERMILION CITY GYM LEADER, USES IT TO TRANSPORT SUPPLIES TO CINNABAR ISLAND...
S.S.ANN
BUT WHAT COULD BE BIG ENOUGH TO...?
OH.
RATTTLE RATTTLE
GLINT
COULD THOSE "SUP-PLIES" BE...?
S.S.ANN
A *SHIPFUL* OF SUPPLIES FOR...A GYM LEADER ?!
OKAY, THEN...
BINGO !!

TIME FOR ME TO TAKE A *CRUISE!*
BAMM
VMM
STOP !!
TAP
TAP TAP
IF YOU MUST GO... I HAVE ONE REQUEST.
GLARE
IT BETTER BE IMPOR-TANT.
WOULD YOU LEAVE PIKACHU BEHIND? FOR ME TO CUDDLE?
TEE HEE
FOMP!
CLUB
WE LOVE POKÉMON
TEE HEE
TAKE CARE
SHEESH
...

PLSH PLSH
SHWOP!
ON THE WATER-FRONT...
S.S. ANNE
WAIT THERE FOR ME, OKAY?
SWSSH
THANKS, BULBA-SAUR!
OKAY. THIS TIME WE GO IN FROM THE *BACK*.
VWIPP VWIP
DON'T TELL ME I JUST IMAGINED IT...
HUH? THERE'S NOTHING HERE?!
KRIII
THIS IS THE ROOM WHERE I SAW THAT...
HEY! A POKÉ BALL!

URRR
VTT VTT VTT VTT VTT VTT
WH-WHAT IS THAT ?!
STOP IT!!
EEE-YAA !!
VTT VTT
POLI-WHIRL-ATTACK !!
WHOOSH
WHSH
VING!
MAN! WHAT KINDA POKÉMON WAS THAT?
HOW YOU DOIN' THERE, POLIWHIRL... ?
...

FUMP
P-POLIWHIRL... WHAT'S WRONG?!
HA HA HA.
I'D SAY IT'S IN SHOCK.
HUH?
WATER CONDUCTS ELECTRICITY WELL.
DOOM
I'M FAMOUS FOR RUNNING A TIGHT SHIP HERE.
WE DEAL WITH TRESPASSERS VERY HARSHLY...
...

S.S. ANNE
HEH
NOT YOUR USUAL CHILD'S PLAY, IS IT, BOY?
SHHHHHHH
11 Buzz Off, Electabuzz!
NOW TELL ME... WHAT ARE YOU DOING ON MY SHIP?
SOMEONE IS STEALING POKÉMON FROM TOWN!
AND I'M GOING TO CATCH THE THIEVES!
WAHAHA
DID YOU HEAR THAT, BOYS?!
YOU THINK WE'RE THE BAD GUYS?

WE'RE *FREEING* THOSE POOR, PAMPERED, CODDLED, UNDER-EVOLVED, OVER-DOMESTICATED POKÉMON!
AND IF WE MAKE A LITTLE PROFIT ON THE SIDE, THAT JUST HELPS US DO OUR GOOD WORK, DOESN'T IT? *BWAHA-HAHAHA!!*
SO IT *IS* YOU...
HEH... GET AS MAD AS YOU WANT, SON...BUT DO YOU REALLY THINK YOU CAN TAKE ALL OF US WITH JUST ONE POKÉMON?
...
GLMP
...
BZZ
I THOUGHT SO. LET'S FINISH THIS!
THIS IS A MEAN ONE.
KLANK
CAN'T EVEN GET IT INTO A POKÉ BALL.
BUT IT MAKES A PERFECT *GUARD DOG!!*
BZ BZZ BZZ BZ
KLANK
KLANK

CHING
ELECTA-BUZZ—ATTACK !!
BZZZZZZZ
BZZZT
BZTBZT
!
BZAMMM
EEP !!
SHHHH
THAT'S JUST A TASTE OF—THE THUNDER-PUNCH!
WHEW
...
WHAT AM I GONNA DO NOW...?!

GRRR...
HEH... THIS TIME HE WON'T MISS...
PLIRP
PLIRP
PLIRP
PLIRP
ELECTABUZZ—ATTACK!!
BUZZ
POLIWHIRL— NOW!
!
WUP
TINK
TINK
TINK
KA-TINK!
!!
ICE?!
GOTCHA!
CHKK

BOM
HEY !!
HAK! HAK!
HAK!
HE... *KOF*... GOT AWAY... !
LITTLE BRAT... THINKS HE CAN OUTSMART ME, EH?

OOOO! THAT WAS WAY TOO CLOSE !

GREAT WORK, POLIWHIRL! JUST LIKE WHEN WE WERE LITTLE...
...AND WERE ALWAYS ESCAPING FROM BULLIES.
HATE TO DO IT, BUT WE GOTTA BAIL FOR NOW.
TP...
?!

MMM
ANOTHER ONE!
MMMM
A MAGNEMITE!
WHILE THEY GO THAT WAY, I'LL...
THEY'RE ALL OVER THE PLACE... AND PROBABLY LOOKING FOR ME!
THIS BETTER NOT BE A TRAP...
ULP... SOMETHING TELLS ME THIS ISN'T EXACTLY THE WAY TO THE EXIT...
?
HA HA HA...

GULP!
!
MMM
MMMM
MWEEEEEEEE E E
GYAAAAA!!!
GOMP
WELL, WELL!
FSSH
NO! POLI-WHIRL!
LT. SURGE!!
HEH HEH HEH...
!

WMMZZZT
WHAT THE—?!
STOP!!
SWSH
ZOOM
FLIP!
SAY GOOD-BYE!
AN ELECTRIC BARRIER STRONGER THAN STEEL! YOU CAN'T GET THROUGH!
WHA HA HA HA HA!!
SPLISH
BZZT BZZTT
WE'LL SHOW YOU WHAT HAPPENS TO LITTLE BOYS WHO GO WHERE THEY SHOULDN'T...
MMMMMM
P... POLI-WHIRL...

ELECTA-BUZZ-
THUNDER-BOLT!!
BZZZZZZZZZZZ
BZZT
HEH...
BZZZT
BZT
BZZT BZZT
YEEEEEE!!
MMMM
THAT SHOULD BE ENOUGH.
FAP
BLOOSH
BON VOYAGE!
...

THIS HAPPENED ONCE BEFORE...
I REMEMBER...
BLUB
BLUB
BLUB
WSSH
BLUB
BLUB
POLIWAG WAS THERE... BUT COULDN'T HELP ME...
BLOOSH
EEK !!
SLIP!
A LONG TIME AGO...
BUT... BUT THEN POLIWAG EVOLVED TO SAVE ME...
SSSSS—
WELL. THAT TAKES CARE OF THAT...
BLUB
BLUB
WSSSHH

WHOOOM
NO !!
A POLIWRATH ?!
WHM
BOM
ELECTA-BUZZ! ATTACK!
BZZZ
BZT BZTT
WHSSH
!
BZTT

BUZZ !!
I...UH... THINK I LEFT THE BATHTUB RUNNING...
BWMMM
...
PPP
PPPPP
M?
@×△#!
NO !!
WHRRR
NOT THE SEISMIC TOSS !!
BMFF

AND SO...
MOVE 'EM OUT, BOYS!
S.S.ANNE
THEY DIDN'T FIND LT. SURGE...
TROMP TROMP
S.S.ANNE
BUT THEY FOUND AND RESCUED **ALL** THE KIDNAPPED POKÉMON!
NOW MY ONLY PROBLEM IS...
MY BOY! MY BOY!
OH... MR. DIRECTOR...
I HEARD ALL ABOUT IT! CONGRATULATIONS, MY BOY! AND THANK YOU!
UH... HEH-HEH... YEAH, BUT...
WHAT'S THIS? YOUR POLIWHIRL! DID IT EVOLVE INTO THIS POLIWRATH ?!
Y-YEAH... BUT IT'S STILL CUTE... ISN'T IT?
WNG WNG
LITTLE POLIWHIRL... *SIGH*

SHAKA SHAKA
SHAKA
BUT WHERE IS MY LITTLE ABRA? TELL ME THE TRUTH!
WHERE? WHERE?! WHERE ?!
W-WELL... YOU SEE...
YOUR LITTLE ABRA... EVOLVED INTO...A GREAT, BIG ALAKAZAM!
EEEEEEEEEEEK!
FOMP
N...NO, NO, NO...
MR. DIRECTO-O-O-OR!
...

SQUEE
SQUEE
ATTENTION ALL POKÉMON TRAINERS!
TAKE YOUR POSITIONS!!
OUR THANKS TO MIRACLE CYCLE FOR SPONSORING THIS RACE...
AND TO ALL OF YOU FOR TAKING PART!
A MERE 10 KILOMETERS ON LEVEL WELL-MARKED ROADS! NOTHING TO IT!
FINISH
ROUTE 12
ROUTE 11
START
AN EASY RACE COURSE!
OF COURSE, ON THE WAY...
WELL...
GIGGLE!
BUT WE SHOULDN'T GIVE AWAY *EVERYTHING*, SHOULD WE?
EVERYONE ON THEIR BIKES?
START
THEN GET READY... GET SET...
GULP!

SSSHHHHHHHH
GO !!
⑫ Wake Up—You're Snorlax!
SSSSHHH
I EVEN PAID A 30-SMACKER ENTRY FEE TO GET INTO THIS RACE...
AUGH! I REALLY WANT THAT FIRST PRIZE...
HUFF
HUFF
SSSSHHHHHHH
NGH
MAYBE BORROWING A BIKE FROM THAT POKÉMON FAN CLUB WASN'T SUCH A GOOD IDEA...
WHAT'S WITH THIS STUPID BIKE?!
BUT I CAN'T GET UP ANY SPEED!
KRIIK KRIIK KRIIK KRIIK
GRRN

EASY! EASY!
HUH ?!
KI//// KI////
SSSHHHHH
OH, GEEZ... LOOK HOW FAR BEHIND I AM!
MAYBE I SHOULD JUST DROP OUT NOW.
BURBLE! BURBLE!
WOBBLE WOBBLE
IT'S JUST A RIVER... WHY'RE YOU CROSSING ONE AT A TIME?
WHY'RE THEY ALL BUNCHED UP HERE?
ACK !
TENTA-CRUEL !!
KROOOL
TAKE A LOOK...
SURE IT IS!
NO WAY! THIS ISN'T FAIR !

THIS ISN'T JUST A RACE! IT'S A POKÉMON OBSTACLE COURSE!
WHOA!
HAVEN'T YOU EVER RACED IN THE TRI-POKÉMON BEFORE?
FOR STARTERS...
AWRIGHT! I CAN WIN THIS THING!
SEE YA!!
BLBLBLBLBBL
AND FOR OBSTACLES LIKE THIS... YOU'RE ALLOWED TO USE YOUR OWN POKÉMON!
POLIWRATH— ICE BEAM BRIDGE!!
WHSH WHSH WHSH
OHH!
BLOOSH
WHAP
GIMME FIVE, POLIWRATH!!
SSSSHHHHHHHH
WHSH WHSH
TINK! TINK!
WHOOSH
WHOA...

WE'VE GAINED A LOTTA GROUND...
SHHHHHHHH
IF WE CAN KEEP GOING LIKE THIS...
SKRHHH
コース
HEY! WHERE DOES THAT GUY THINK HE'S GOING?
OH, WELL! THAT'S HIS PROBLEM! I'M ONE OBSTACLE CLOSER TO—
ERK
DOOOOOOOM
A FOREST !!
RACE
A THICK ONE, TOO.
NO WAY I CAN RIDE THROUGH THAT...
NO WONDER EVERYBODY ELSE IS GOING AROUND IT.
GUESS I'LL JUST HAVE TO DO THE SAME...
SHWIIIII

YOU'RE GOING THROUGH THERE...?
I KNOW A SHORTCUT!
PSSHHHH
HEY!
DON'T TRY IT.
YES!
WAHAHA! ANOTHER CHANCE TO MOVE UP!
OH YEAH?
PSSHHHH
THE FOREST IS INFESTED WITH BUG POKÉMON.
IT'LL BE A LONG-CUT FOR YOU!
KRNN
LET'S GO!
WHO'S AFRAID OF SOME BUGS?!
KSSH
IF YOU DON'T HAVE BUG SPRAY, YOU BETTER STAY OUT.
SEE YA!

SHHHHHHHHH
PXX
PXX
OH YEAH!
PXX
I'VE GOT AN ELECTRIC POKÉMON THAT'LL FRY 'EM ALL!
HEY, BULBASAUR! OPEN A PATH WITH YOUR RAZOR LEAF!
SWRRRRRRR
THIS RACE IS *OURS*!
SWRRRRRRR
SWISH!
BONK!
HUH?

BLORG
A BEEDRILL'S HIVE!
!!
BEEEEEEEEE
AIEEEEEE!!!
BEEEEEEEEEE
AND THAT MEANS...
WOBBLE OBBLE
EVERY SHORTCUT... HAS A BIIIIIIG PRICE...
KLUNK
OWWWW...
B-BUT LOOK WHERE WE ARE !!

LAST LEG, GUYS!! LET'S ROLL!!
YOU'VE BEEN GREAT, BUT FROM HERE ON, THIS IS MY RACE!
I'M GONNA WIN THIS MYSELF!
AND THEY'RE APPROACHING THE FINISH LINE!
BATTLING FOR THE LEAD ARE SWIMMER AND BUG CATCHER!
WHILE A SURPRISING THIRD IS THIS YOUNGSTER!
WHICH OF THEM WILL BE THE WINNER?
1ST PRIZE
WHO WILL BE THE ONE TO TAKE HOME ALL THESE POKÉMON ITEMS AND 10,000 IN PRIZE MONEY?!
SHHHHHHH

ROUTE 12 FISHING PIER..
WHAT THE HECK IS THAT?
WHAT'S GOIN' ON?
LOOKS LIKE WE'RE TIED...FOR NOTHING!
WE'LL NEVER GET PAST THIS!
WEIRD.
DOOOM
HOW'D A BOULDER GET OUT HERE?
WAK! IT'S A SNORLAX!!!
THEY CAN SLEEP FOREVER! NOTHING WAKES THEM UP!
ZZZZ
ZZZZ
ZZ

THEN WE'LL JUST HAVE TO CAPTURE IT!
WHRRR
POLIWRATH, I CHOOSE YOU!!
PLONG
?!
WHHRRRR
PLONNNG
THE SNORLAX SLEEPS RIGHT THROUGH IT!
?!
REEEEN
HP
YOU THINK WE DIDN'T TRY ALREADY?
NO MATTER WHAT WE DO...
20

WELL, HERE GOES NOTHING...
FOOD...
OH-HO-HO... SO THAT'S HOW IT IS...
ONLY ONE THING'LL WAKE UP A SNORLAX... **FOOD!**
ZZZZZZ
HEY, **SNORLAX!** HOW 'BOUT A **SNACK?!**
...
IT'S OKAY, BULBASAUR! I PROMISE!
WHAT?!
SNRRRR?

SNRLLL
COME ON, CAN'T YOU SMELL IT...? IT'S BEEDRILL HONEY...
WAFT WAFT
LAXX!

SOON...
I CAN SEE THE LEADERS APPROACHING!
CAN'T MAKE THEM OUT YET...
FINISH
THERE THEY ARE! LET'S HEAR SOME CHEERS FOR OUR NEXT WIN–
D-DM D-DM D-DM D-DM D-DM D-DM D-DM D-DM
HUH?
THAT'S NOT A BIKE!
D-DM D-DM D-DM D-DM

DOOM
WHAT...
...IS THAT THING?!
SHHHHHHH
DGOOOOOM
FINISH
AND TH-THE WINNER IS...
YAAAGH!!
I CAN'T BE-LIEVE IT...
THE 10,000 IN PRIZE MONEY...
AND IT TOOK EVERY CENT TO FILL UP THIS STUPID SNORLAX!
SOBB!
GOBBLE
GOBBLE

13 Sigh for Psyduck
SSSSHHHHHHHH
UP NORTH, IN LAVENDER TOWN...
GYAAAAAAA!!
WE'VE GOTTA FIND A PLACE TO GET OUT OF THIS RAIN!
SSSHHHHHHH
UM... EXCUSE ME...
FWIP
...
'SCUSE ME... !
LET'S TRY THAT AGAIN.
FWIP
...
GEEZ! IS THIS "LAVENDER" TOWN OR "LEAVE 'EM THERE" TOWN?

NOT VERY TRUSTING PEOPLE, ARE THEY?
GASP
EEEE-YAAAA!
HOW DID HE SNEAK UP ON ME LIKE THAT?!
SSSHHHHH
UM...MIND IF I ASK WHAT YOU'RE DOING?
HO, HO. JUST PAYING MY RESPECTS.
HE LIVED TO A RIPE OLD AGE, MY BELOVED POKÉMON...
DODUO REST IN PEACE
BUT HIS TIME CAME AT LAST.
...
THANK YOU.
VIP
ARE YOU ALSO FOND OF POKÉ-MON?
COME. HAVE SOMETHING WARM TO DRINK AT MY HOUSE.
SSSHHHHH

RMM RMM
THE HOME OF MR. FUJI...
SSSHHHH
KLUG KLUG
FOR MANY YEARS, THIS TOWN WAS SAID TO BE A GATHERING PLACE FOR THE SOULS OF POKÉMON.
RMM
TO HONOR THE SOULS... AND GIVE THEM A PLACE OF REST...THE TOWNSPEOPLE ERECTED A GREAT POKÉMON TOWER.
Y'MEAN... THAT BUILDING IS A POKÉMON... CEMETERY?
INDEED.
SSSHHHH
BUT IF THAT'S THE CEMETERY, WHY DIDN'T YOU BUILD YOUR MEMORIAL THERE?
BECAUSE NO ONE DARES VENTURE NEAR THE TOWER! WHENEVER WE RISK IT...
...THEY APPEAR.
"THEY"...?
THE GHOSTS...

G-G-GHOSTS?!
WAAA-HA-HA-HA-HA!! GHOSTS, HE SAYS! POKÉMON GHOSTS!!
YOU SAW THE FEAR IN THE TOWNSPEOPLE'S EYES FOR YOURSELF...
THEY'VE BECOME SO TERRIFIED OF THE GHOSTS THAT THEY HAVE FORGOTTEN HOW TO TRUST ONE ANOTHER.
THEY WON'T EVEN MAKE EYE CONTACT WITH STRANGERS!
BUT YOU MAY CHOOSE TO BELIEVE... OR NOT.
FLIP
IS THAT... YOUR DODUO?
IT WAS.
IF ONLY I COULD LET MY POKÉMON REST IN A PROPER PLACE INSTEAD OF A WEED-GROWN ALLEY...
YOU MUST'VE CARED A LOT FOR YOUR DODUO...
FLIP

I'M ON A QUEST TO FILL THIS POKÉDEX WITH INFORMATION ON EVERY POKÉMON THERE IS...
YOU KNOW THAT LAD?!
BL-BL-BL-BL-BLUE?!
!!
...AND MY RIVAL ON THAT QUEST IS BLUE!!
GULP
JUST LIKE YOU, WHEN I TOLD HIM ABOUT THE GHOSTS, HE LAUGHED IT OFF...
WHERE IS HE NOW?!
AH... HE PASSED THROUGH TOWN JUST BEFORE I LOST MY DODUO...
!
BUT THEN, IN RECENT TIMES... NO ONE WHO ENTERS THE TOWER EVER COMES OUT AGAIN!
!
HE RAN OFF TO THE TOWER TO SHOW UP OUR FOOLISHNESS. THAT WAS TWO WEEKS AGO. HE HASN'T COME BACK.

THE GUY'S PERSONALITY COULD USE SOME IMPROVEMENT, BUT AS A POKÉMON TRAINER HE'S THE REAL THING. HE DOESN'T GO DOWN EASY!
RMMM
RMMM
SO BLUE IS MIS-SING...
SO WHAT COULD PUT HIM OUT OF ACTION FOR TWO WEEKS...?
COULD IT POS-SIBLY BE...?
SPSH
COULD THAT TOWER REALLY BE HAUNTED BY GHOSTS...?!
...
GLARE
ZZZM
WELL, I'M NOT RUNNING AWAY FROM A CHALLENGE THAT HE TOOK ON!
I'LL FIND OUT THE TRUTH BEHIND THOSE "GHOSTS" !!

VREEEEEE
HHSSSSHHHH
BRRRR
GLLP
PLOP
!
EEP!
YAAAAAAA
PLIP
F-FOOEY... JUST WATER DR-DRIPPING...
GOTTA GET A GRIP!
BUT MAN... THIS PLACE DIDN'T LOOK SO HUGE FROM THE OUTSIDE! WH-WHERE'S THE OTHER...
HHSSSS
HEY... WHAT'S WITH THIS FOG...?

HUH?
HOOOO
IS THAT A POKÉMON?
M-MORE OF 'EM!
HWOOO
SSSHHHHH
HOOO
HOO
GRAAA
HEEEE-YOOOOW!!

A G-G-G-GHOST !!
AIEE!
BOM
BU-BULBASAUR !
RAZOR LEAF—NOW!
BWRRRRRRRR
SORP!
N-N-NOTHING... ?
SSHHHHHHH
WE GOTTA STOP THESE THINGS! BULBASAUR!
SLEEP POW-DER !
BLLP

SHAAAA A
BLBB
BLBB
THIS SHOULD DO IT...
GLMP!
SSHHHHHHHHH
NO!
IT DIDN'T EVEN SLOW 'EM DOWN!
HWOOO
THEY'RE GHOSTS!! NOTHING HAS ANY EFFECT!!
WHAT AM I GONNA DO...?!
YEEE!
SWIP!
BNNG
GASP!
IT'S... IT'S...
NNG

TNNG
ZZLORP
TNNG
...FALLING APART!
KRAK
SNAP
SSHHH
FFF
FFF
GLAKK
IT'S JUST...AN EMPTY SHELL...
BUT WHAT WAS MAKING IT MOVE...?
WHO'S **CONTROLLING** THESE THINGS?!
HWOOOO
HOOO
...
TRYIN' TO ***MIST***-IFY ME, EH?! WELL—
HOOO

SHH
GLAAGH!
SHHHH
RAR!
VMMM
BULBA-SAUR! RUN FOR IT!
HUH?
HOO? HOO?
THEY'RE NOT FOL-LOWING US...?
WAIT A SECOND... NONE OF 'EM ARE LEAVING THE FOG!
HWOOO
THAT MUST MEAN...
HHHSSSSSSS S
THIS PURPLE HAZE IS WHAT'S CONTROLLING THOSE ZOMBIES!!
ALL RIGHT! NOW THAT I KNOW *THAT*...

PM!!
?!
CHOOMF
KRAKL
COULD IT BE THAT...?
FIRE?!
FSH!
ACK! YEOWCH!
YOU'RE OKAY!! I NEVER THOUGHT I'D BE GLAD TO SAY THAT!!
RMM
NOW LET'S—
HOOOOO
BL- BLUE!!

CHOOSH
?!
...
?
WHAT'S THE IDEA, YOU...
RRR
HENHH
HHHSSS SSSHHH
BLUE? WHAT HAPPENED TO YOU?!

14 That Awful Arbok!

BLAPF
WE CAN'T FIGHT EACH OTHER... WE'VE GOTTA FIGURE OUT WHO'S BEHIND ALL THIS!!
BNNG...
THERE'S ONLY ONE POKÉMON I KNOW WHO CAN TAKE OVER BODIES LIKE THIS...
HOOOOOOO
ONE GAS POKÉMON WITH PSYCHIC ABILITIES... GASTLY!
THAT'S WHO WE GOTTA TAKE DOWN!!
BLSH
BULBASAUR—ATTACK GASTLY!!
SHHH...
HUH?
SH...
OH, NO!

GASTLY'S MADE OF GAS! THE RAZOR LEAVES GO RIGHT THROUGH... !
OH, GREAT! CHAR-MELEON'S FIRE SPIN!
CHHOOOOOSHH
HENH
B-B-B-B-B-B-B
BBWWRRRRRRR
?!
SSSSHHHHHH
...?!
FFFF
SHIMP
SHIMP

BWOOOOOO!
WAY TO GO, BULBASAUR! KEEP IT UP 'TIL YOU HEAR A *GASTLY* "BLORP"!
BLORP!
SSSHHH—
YOU AIN'T *SEED* NOTHIN' YET! *WA-HA!*
YOU THOUGHT THAT PLANT ON ITS BACK COULD ONLY SPEW THINGS *OUT*?
DMMM
SSHHHHHHHHH
PPFFFFF
BLUP
NNNNH!!
YOO-HOO, BLUE! SNAP OUT OF IT!
FUMP
WHOA.
PFFF...

HUH?
OH. IT'S JUST YOU.
AH! BACK TO YOUR OLD OBNOXIOUS SELF, I SEE!
WHEW!
THAT'S RIGHT! YOU HAVE MY GRATITUDE FOR TODAY, OF COURSE... AND NOW THAT THAT'S OVER WITH...
PAP! PAP!
...
BLUE, WE GOTTA GET OUTTA THIS TOWER! SOMETHING'S REALLY WRONG H—
HEY! THAT'S NOT AN EXIT! I SAID, WE GOTTA GET OUTTA—
I'LL SHOW THAT BUFFOON!
"BUFFOON"...?
THINKS HE CAN CAST A SPELL ON *ME*, DOES HE...?

HEEEY! WAIT UP!
I DIDN'T ASK YOU TO TAG ALONG.
HUFF HUFF
I TAKE BACK THAT *"OLD OBNOXIOUS SELF"* LINE! YOU'RE WORSE!
I JUST FINISHED FIGHTING A WHOLE HORDE OF ZOMBIES...
...TO SAVE ***YOUR*** STUPID HIDE AND NOW—
FEH!
YES. AND I EX-PRESSED MY GRATI-TUDE.
SHEESH... HOW TALL IS THIS TOWER ANYWAY?!
HUH?
BLP...
WHAT'S THIS STUFF...?
AARB
EEYAAAAA!!

VISH!
BLORK
ARRBL
BWOP!
!
NYAHAHAHA!!
SHOW YOUR-SELF!
THAT'S A POISON POKÉMON'S VENOM. PAY ATTENTION OR YOU'LL END UP AS YOGURT!
SHHH
GAAA!!
HA HA HA...
S——H
heh
AH, YES. THE SQUIRT WHO SPOILED MY CAREFULLY LAID PLANS.
YOU! THE ONE FROM MT. MOON!

I AM ONE OF TEAM ROCKET'S ELITE TRIAD...
NINJA KOGA!
AS IF TEAM ROCKET HAD AN ELITE ANYTHING!
WOULDN'T YOU THINK A TEAM OF EVILDOERS COULD BUILD A BASE WITHOUT ALL THESE ANNOYING INTERRUPTIONS?
YOU MEAN THIS TOWER-?!
IT'S PERFECT FOR US—SINCE THE SIMPLE TOWNSFOLK BLAME EVERYTHING SUSPICIOUS ON GHOSTS!
CHARMELEON—ATTACK!!
CHWOOOOOSH
SSS
JUST A PROJECTION?!

AAAABOK
AND YOU WERE COMPLAINING ABOUT BEING A ZOMBIE SLAVE!
IF YOU'D JUST STAYED THAT WAY, YOU WOULDN'T HAVE TO DIE NOW!
!!
YOW!
BLOOOOOOSH
RBLLL
WHERE D'YOU THINK YOU'RE GOIN'?!
FOLLOW ME—IF YOU FEEL LIKE SEEING TOMORROW!
AAARB
KKKKK
ZOOM

BLK
VROOM
ARE YOU *NUTS?!* YOU'RE HEADIN' RIGHT BACK TOWARD THE ZOMBIES!!
...
KOGA'S CON-TROLLING HIS POKÉMON FROM A DISTANCE...
WHICH MEANS...
ARR!
FWIP
CHAR-MELEON-REFLECT!
CHWOO!
KRAKL
KRAKKL
KRASH

BWAT
BWAT
BWAT
...
FORGET IT! NOT EVEN FIRE CAN STOP ARBOK'S ACID!
KRAKL KRAKL
SO...THE "REFLECT" DEFENSE...
KR-KRAK
NYA-HA-HA-HA-HA!!
SSSSSSSSSSS
BLOX
!

CHASH
WHAT ?!
WHAT THE ZOMBIE ARBOK MELTED... WAS JUST ONE OF ITS MASTER'S ZOMBIES!
SSSSSSSSSS
A TRAINER WOULD'VE SEEN THAT EASILY... IF HE'D *BEEN* HERE.
BLKK
OO. THIS BLUE IS GOOD. NOT THAT I'LL *EVER* TELL HIM THAT...
BONK
RRB
RRB

BWAT
BWAT
BWAT
BWAT
AAARA
GRRRR...
I WON'T FORGET THIS, LITTLE WORMS!
HEAVE...HO!
THERE YOU ARE, RED.
THANKS TO YOU, THIS TOWN HAS A LIFE AGAIN.

DODUO
AND MY LITTLE ONE WILL REST EASY AT LAST.
AW, GEEZ... I WISH I COULD TELL YOU I DID IT.
BUT HE'S THE ONE YOU'VE GOTTA THANK!
OKAY, GUYS! LET'S ROLL!
To be continued in the next volume...

COMING SOON IN VOLUME 2!
GROAAR
VWOOSH
AND WHY IS SHE AFTER RED?
WHAT IS CAUSING A DISTURBANCE IN THE RANKS OF TEAM ROCKET?!
YOU WON'T BE ABLE TO PUT THIS VOLUME DOWN!!
GOTCHA!
WHO IS THIS MYSTERIOUS GIRL?
A MONSTROUS EXPERIMENT!
GLOP...
GLUP
POKÉMON ADVENTURES VOLUME 2!!
AH NO... THAT SQUIRTLE IS... WELL...
PLUS... A LEGENDARY POKÉMON...?!
FLASH!
DON'T MISS IT!!

ALL!
ADVENTURE ROUTE MAP 1
VS FEAROW
POOM
!
FOLLOW RED ON HIS QUEST TO COMPLETE THE POKEDEX! THIS IS HOW FAR HE GOT IN VOLUME 1!
SEA COTTAGE
CHAPTER 8
CHAPTER 9
CERULEAN CITY
ADVENTURE ROUTE
DWOSH!
VS PSYDUCK
VS ARBOK
CHAPTERS 13 AND 14
LAVENDER TOWN
CHAPTERS 10 AND 11
VERMILION CITY
VS MEW
ROUTES 11, 12 AND 13
CHAPTER 12
GRAB
VS SNORLAX
DMDMDMDMDM
WHAT IS THAT?
WHOA!
VS STARMIE
WHPSH
IS THAT YOUR BEST?
IT'S NOT GOING TO WORK!
VS VOLTORB
VS ELECTRABUZZ
THIS IS THE PATH I FOLLOWED!!

GOTTA CATCH 'EM
GOTTA CATCH 'EM ALL!
ADVENTURE ROUTE MAP 1
CHAPTER 7
MT. MOON
ROUTE 3
CHAPTER 6
PEWTER CITY
CHAPTERS 4 AND 5
CHAPTER 3
VIRIDIAN FOREST
CHAPTER 2
VIRIDIAN CITY
CHAPTER 1
PALLET TOWN
GGAAH
VS RHYDON
GYROOOAAR
VS GYARADOS
BZZAP BZAP ZAP
BAM
VS PIKACHU
VS ONIX
VS KANGASKHAN
BOOM
CRACK CRUSH CRACK
VS MACHOKE

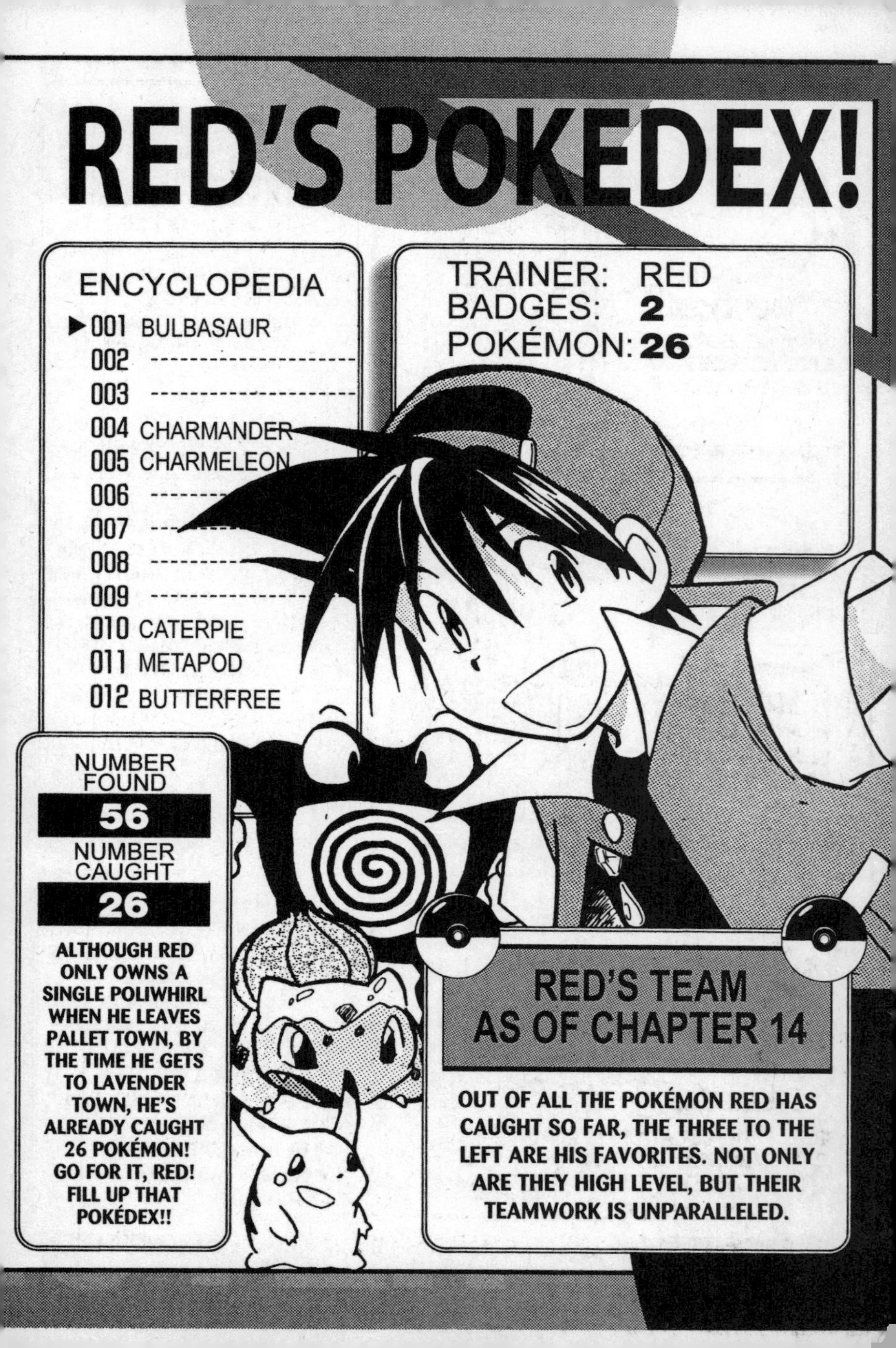
RED'S POKEDEX!
ENCYCLOPEDIA
▶001 BULBASAUR
002 --------------------
003 --------------------
004 CHARMANDER
005 CHARMELEON
006 ---------
007 ---------
008 ---------
009 --------------------
010 CATERPIE
011 METAPOD
012 BUTTERFREE
TRAINER: RED
BADGES: 2
POKÉMON: 26
NUMBER FOUND
56
NUMBER CAUGHT
26
ALTHOUGH RED ONLY OWNS A SINGLE POLIWHIRL WHEN HE LEAVES PALLET TOWN, BY THE TIME HE GETS TO LAVENDER TOWN, HE'S ALREADY CAUGHT 26 POKÉMON! GO FOR IT, RED! FILL UP THAT POKÉDEX!!
RED'S TEAM AS OF CHAPTER 14
OUT OF ALL THE POKÉMON RED HAS CAUGHT SO FAR, THE THREE TO THE LEFT ARE HIS FAVORITES. NOT ONLY ARE THEY HIGH LEVEL, BUT THEIR TEAMWORK IS UNPARALLELED.

PIKACHU: L21

PIKACHU WAS CAUGHT WHILE IT WAS UP TO NO GOOD IN PEWTER CITY. BEFORE THAT, IT LIVED IN VIRIDIAN FOREST. AT FIRST, PIKACHU WAS STUBBORN AND DIDN'T WANT TO LISTEN TO RED, BUT NOW THEY ARE INSEPARABLE FRIENDS. PIKACHU'S SPECIALTIES ARE THE THUNDER WAVE, THUNDERBOLT, AND OTHER POWERFUL ELECTRIC ATTACKS!

/ 85

STATE/NORMAL

NO.001

TYPE1/GRASS
EXPERIENCE POINTS/**27000**
TRAINER/ RED

RED RECEIVED THIS POKÉMON AS A GIFT FROM PROFESSOR OAK. IT HAS A CALM PERSONALITY AND, EVEN THOUGH IT HASN'T GROWN UP AROUND OTHER POKÉMON, IT MATURES RAPIDLY DURING ITS TRAVELS WITH RED! RED'S BULBASAUR IS NOW A VETERAN FIGHTER WHO USES ATTACKS LIKE VINE WHIP AND LEECH SEED IN BATTLE!

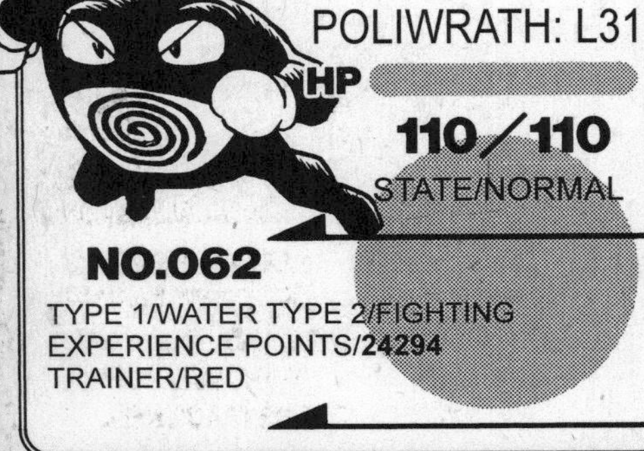

POLIWRATH: L31

HP

110 / 110

STATE/NORMAL

NO.062

TYPE 1/WATER TYPE 2/FIGHTING
EXPERIENCE POINTS/**24294**
TRAINER/RED

RED BEFRIENDED THIS POKÉMON WHEN HE WAS A TODDLER. YEARS AGO, IT EVOLVED FROM A POLIWAG INTO A POLIWHIRL AND FINALLY—DURING THEIR RECENT TRAVELS—INTO A POLIWRATH. NOW "FIGHTING TYPE" COMPLEMENTS ITS "WATER TYPE." WITH ITS ENHANCED COMBAT SKILLS, POLIWRATH MOVES SEAMLESSLY ALONGSIDE RED IN BATTLE!

Message from
Hidenori Kusaka

Whenever I write, I always have this goal in mind: to express in manga form the surprise and wonder that one feels while playing the Pokémon games. I always think to myself, "Perhaps this Pokémon lives in a place like this. Or maybe this Pokémon's attack looks like that." And now, the result of these and many other musings have been collected into a first volume! So let's begin our journey with Red as he embarks on a quest to complete his Pokédex!!

THIS IS THE END OF THIS GRAPHIC NOVEL!

To properly enjoy this VIZ Media graphic novel, please turn it around and begin reading from right to left.

This book has been printed in the original Japanese format in order to preserve the orientation of the original artwork. Have fun with it!

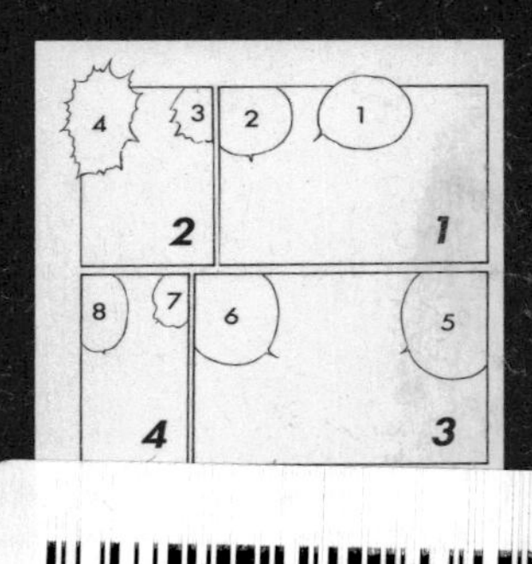